Bride *and* Seek

Janet Holm McHenry

Annie's®
AnniesFiction.com

Books in the Antique Shop Mysteries series

Library of Congress-in-Publication Data
Bride and Seek / by Janet Holm McHenry
p. cm.
I. Title
                    2017949579

AnniesFiction.com
(800) 282-6643
Antique Shop Mysteries™
Series Creator: Shari Lohner
Series Editor: Elizabeth Morrissey
Cover Illustrator: Bonnie Leick

10 11 12 13 14 | Printed in South Korea | 9 8 7 6

"Snickers? Where did you go this time?" Maggie Watson headed up her curved staircase to the second-floor landing. When she had started the vacuum half an hour ago, her lovable tabby, Snickers, had hightailed it upstairs to an unknown location. Sedgwick Manor—the nineteenth-century Colonial Revival mansion in Somerset Harbor, Maine, that Maggie and Snickers called home—offered nearly endless places where a cat could hide out from a mean cleaning machine. And now that it was nearly summer, he could just as easily hightail it outside as well.

The storage bedroom door stood slightly ajar, and Maggie stepped through. "Hiding in here again?" She knew that Snickers would come out eventually, but she was hoping he would come out sooner rather than later to snuggle with her while she read a book in the library. Not that Snickers ever did anything on any terms but his own.

Dressed for cleaning in jeans, a cotton pullover, and sneakers, Maggie slowly scanned the room's stacks of storage boxes and sheet-covered antiques. No feline to be found amid the covered dresser, vanity, or side tables. "Snickers, where are you?"

She walked to the window and peeked behind the curtain. *Not there*, she thought.

Then she heard a muffled crash from the other side of the bedroom wall. *Oh, Snickers.*

With a pretty good idea of what had caused the racket, she walked back out the bedroom door and strode to the nearby guest suite, through its bathroom, and into a large walk-in closet, where she discovered the sight she had expected: a pile of cardboard shoe boxes lay in a jumble on the floor, their lids askew and their contents spilling onto the rug.

"Aha, there you are." At the sound of Maggie's voice, Snickers cracked one eye from his perch on a hatbox on the top shelf in the room-size closet. "Come on down, you silly thing, before you make a bigger mess."

Snickers yawned and stretched for a long moment to remind her that he didn't take orders, then jumped into Maggie's outstretched arms. She stroked his tan, white, and brown fur as she surveyed the landscape of hanging clothes. She had inherited it all a few years earlier when her aunt Evelyn had passed away and made Maggie the new owner of Sedgwick Manor and the adjacent antiques shop, Carriage House Antiques.

Maybe there was a good reason for Snickers hiding out. He had reminded her that she still hadn't sorted through all of her aunt's personal belongings, some of which still held a hint of Evelyn's Arpège perfume. Maggie had brought many of the shoe boxes, hatboxes, and hanging suits, dresses, and garment bags upstairs long ago when she had moved into the manor's first-floor bedroom suite.

What a process it had been to combine her possessions with Aunt Evelyn's. Plain pots and pans had been easy to donate to her church, Old Faith Chapel, for its annual tag sale. But she hadn't wanted to purge any items with memories attached to them, so most had collected dust in dark closet corners like this one.

Maybe now is finally the time to sort through the clothing. It'll only show more age as the months or years go by. Perhaps some of the clothes, shoes, hats, and jewelry could be sold in Carriage House Antiques or given to the church ladies for the tag sale.

Maggie put Snickers down when he began to squirm, then

turned her attention to the closet's contents. First, she tidied up the mess Snickers had made and carried the shoe boxes to the guest suite bed. Then, one by one, she brought the petite suits and dresses from earlier decades to join the shoes, laying them in separate piles for Carriage House Antiques and the Old Faith Chapel tag sale.

As Maggie eyed a navy-blue wool dress with white piping that likely dated to the 1950s, she thought of the new vintage clothing store that was opening soon near The Quilt Cupboard, her friend Fran's quilt shop. Word around town was that an older woman was the mastermind behind A Fine Vintage, and Maggie wondered if perhaps the proprietor would be interested in purchasing some of Aunt Evelyn's clothing from bygone days. Recalling the sign in the storefront window advertising an opening day reception, she thought that might be the perfect opportunity to talk to the new owner.

Maggie chuckled as she imagined some of Aunt Evelyn's sayings that would be perfect signs for a thrift store.

"It makes sense to save your cents!"

"Look to the past to save for the future!"

"A penny saved is a penny you could spend on your new favorite antique!"

Maggie and Evelyn had shared an affection for the past, which was why her aunt had bequeathed her the house, the shop, and the contents of both—including the treasury of old clothing that Maggie was currently categorizing. She returned her attention to the task at hand. *Okay, where should all this go?*

A two-piece tweed suit reminiscent of Jackie Kennedy would go to Carriage House Antiques.

Half a dozen cardigans in as many colors were set aside for the Old Faith Chapel tag sale.

A couple of cotton shifts would find their way to the thrift store.

After about an hour of sorting and reminiscing about her aunt wearing this dress or that skirt, only a few long hanging dress bags remained in the back corner of the closet.

Maggie opened the closest bag and found a midcalf charcoal-gray wool coat. She tried it on and found that it fit perfectly. *Maybe I'll keep this for myself.*

The next couple of bags held jeweled evening gowns, and Maggie guessed that Aunt Evelyn had worn them on the Mediterranean cruise she had indulged in a few years before her death. *Would these sell in the shop? I'd better ask June.*

June McGillis had quickly become Maggie's closest friend in Somerset Harbor. The multitalented and energetic strawberry-blonde with a megawatt smile had managed Carriage House Antiques for over a decade. Thanks to her ability to sniff out valuable antiques at yard sales, her knack for smart bidding at auctions, and her eye for creating memorable displays, June was Maggie's invaluable right-hand woman. She used her natural sense of style to create inviting settings in the shop and employed her warm personality to make each customer feel at home. June would find a way to make the sparkly gowns irresistible to buyers.

Maggie returned her focus to the nearly empty closet rod. *Just one more hanging dress package.* The word *package* came to mind because the item was wrapped from top to bottom in a sort of butcher paper that had yellowed over the years—probably decades, from the look of it. Maggie slid the hanger toward her on the wooden rod and carefully pulled the paper apart at the shoulder areas, then let it fall to the closet floor.

Her mouth dropped.

Before her hung a stunning off-white satin dress. Layers of scallops the width of her hand covered the gown, and delicate gold beading and embroidery decorated the square neckline.

Based on the tea-length dress's delicate fringed hem, Maggie guessed it dated to the 1920s, and she thought perhaps it could have been a wedding dress.

It was perfect . . . and that was perfectly odd, because its flawlessness indicated that it had never been worn. Was there a flapper bride-to-be who hadn't made it to the altar? And why was this dress in Aunt Evelyn's closet?

Perhaps Maggie could find a reference to it somewhere in Aunt Evelyn's journal. Most of what she had jotted down there was information about her various antique finds—how and where she had acquired them and what she knew of their history. Some furniture in Sedgwick Manor and Carriage House Antiques could be traced back to the Revolutionary War and even Colonial times. Would Maggie find something in Evelyn's notes about this mysterious bridal gown?

The thought of the journal made Maggie's longing for her aunt more acute. Evelyn had reminded Maggie of her own mother, Annette, who had passed away many years before. Both of them had been strong, determined women, and they had inspired the same in Maggie.

Another trait Maggie and her aunt had in common was a penchant for mysteries. Maggie found that since moving to Sedgwick Manor, she'd had a habit of getting roped into situations that exercised her previously undiscovered talents as an amateur sleuth. It certainly kept life interesting for her in quaint Somerset Harbor.

And one more mystery was right in front of her. Maggie scrutinized the never-used wedding dress and tried to imagine what it was doing in this closet. What scenario actually made sense? As much as she tried, Maggie couldn't quite picture anyone in Somerset Harbor wearing a wedding dress so trendy for its time. The Jazz Age had centered in metropolitan areas such as New York City. Small towns in Maine had remained fairly traditional, although Maggie knew there were certainly exceptions to every rule.

She checked the garment label. *Wow—Jean Patierre, a well-known designer of the early twentieth century.* This was a treasure, and a valuable one at that.

What to do with it? It was too special to give away to charity or the new A Fine Vintage. And it could have personal family connections, so it didn't seem right to just put a price tag on it in Carriage House Antiques. Someone in the family—maybe even Maggie's daughter, Emily—might like to wear it down the aisle someday.

"Or maybe I'll wear it myself to a costume ball," Maggie said to Snickers.

Maggie slid the dress off the hanger and took it into the guest suite bedroom, where a full-length mirror hung next to the door to the hallway. Pinching the shoulder seams, she held it in front of her and admired the reflection. The boxy style could fit any manner of figure, but it did seem this particular dress was made for someone taller, like Maggie. *Well, why not?*

A few minutes later, Maggie had the dress on. She fluffed her blonde hair, then grabbed her cell phone out of the pocket of her jeans, which were draped across the bed. Although she didn't typically take photos of herself, Maggie clicked a few as she stood in front of the mirror. *Emily will get a kick out of this.* She sent the best of the bunch to her daughter, who always enjoyed seeing Maggie's latest finds.

On a whim, she dialed Emily's number. *Maybe there's a chance she's available to chat.* Not long ago, her daughter had walked across the stage at Saint Joseph's College in Standish, Maine, with her nursing school diploma in hand. Ever the go-getter, Emily had stepped right into a job at Massachusetts General Hospital in Boston—but Maggie might be able to catch her between shifts.

"Hi, Mom."

"Hi, sweetie. Did you get my text? Just wait until you see what I found—"

Before Maggie could get any further, Emily cut in. "Sorry, Mom, I can't really talk. I'm pulling a double shift today and I'm just on a quick break to grab a bite."

"No problem. I'm surprised you picked up."

"I did want to tell you that everything came together on that studio apartment, and I'm signing the lease tomorrow."

Maggie smiled. Emily had worked hard to find the right place close enough to the hospital that she could walk to work. "That's wonderful. I know you said it was tiny, but it's yours, and that means a lot."

"I'm so excited I won't have to sleep on my friends' couch anymore. I'll call you tonight or maybe tomorrow after I sign, okay? And you can tell me about your latest find. Love you, Mom."

About twenty seconds after the call was disconnected, Emily texted her: *What? Okay, we've got to talk!*

Maggie had to laugh. Apparently Emily had seen the photo of her in the wedding dress. She hoped the picture would entice Emily to call her back sooner rather than later, though preferably after the girl got a chance to rest up. *How do nurses go without sleep?* Maggie sighed and returned the phone to her jeans pocket. Seemingly, as quickly as the click of a photo, her little girl had grown up.

After changing out of the gown, Maggie walked to the closet to hang the dress back up. As she did, however, she noticed there was more than just yellowed butcher paper piled up on the closet floor.

She leaned over and picked up a matching fingertip-length veil the same color as the dress. It was as stunning as its counterpart. An off-white cap was trimmed with scalloped satin and lace layers, and a white sequined flower was positioned off to one side. However, Maggie gasped as she looked at it more closely. The single layer of silk tulle was torn from bottom to top.

The torn veil reminded Maggie of a classic romantic novel Emily had done a paper on in high school. She vaguely recalled something about an ordinary young governess falling in love with a brooding gentleman and the young woman's wedding veil being ripped from bottom to top. *What was the name of that book, the name of the author?* She would probably remember it in a day or so. *Then maybe I'll take time to read it for myself.*

As she ran her fingers lightly over the veil, Maggie sighed and wondered what could possibly have happened for the tulle to be torn but the dress to remain unworn.

Was there an argument?

Had love vanished?

Maybe the groom had left the bride at the altar.

Maggie chuckled. She had happened upon many fascinating finds in Sedgwick Manor since moving in, but nothing quite like this. If the dress was from the 1920s, perhaps family ruin at the end of that decade divided two otherwise happy people and set them on separate courses.

After changing back into her jeans and sweater, Maggie put the wedding dress and veil back on the hanger. It didn't seem right to just put them back in the dark closet, so she decided to bring them down to her master suite. As she headed toward the stairs, she held the hanger high to keep both dress and veil off the floor. When she stepped into the hallway, Snickers emerged from another room and looked curiously at the dress.

Maggie could tell by the way he cocked his head that he thought the swaying dress was a new toy. He even reached toward the hem's enticing fringe with a paw as Maggie passed him and headed down the staircase. "Don't even think about it, young man." Snickers wasn't much for games, but apparently he was as intrigued by this discovery as she was—even if it was for an entirely different reason.

In the sitting area of her master suite, she placed the hanger over the top of the door, just out of the cat's reach. She contemplated the best way to get to the bottom of this fresh mystery. Certainly, one of her friends in the Somerset Harbor Historical Society might know something about it. For now, though, Maggie thought she'd ask Maura O'Brien, the head librarian at the town library and a valuable resource for local history. Perhaps she could point Maggie toward information related to the original ownership of the dress. As a bonus, Maggie figured, Maura could also help her remember the name of that novel with the mysterious veil.

Maggie dialed the library as she gazed out the window at the green trees swaying in a gentle breeze on this warm, sunny day.

"Somerset Harbor Library, Maura speaking."

Maggie greeted Maura and then described the dress and veil she had found.

"Torn from the bottom up?" Maura asked. "Sounds like a Brontë plot twist. I never heard of any 1920s weddings planned for Sedgwick Manor or its inhabitants, scandalous or otherwise. But why don't you come down and browse some books on fashion and history? You might find some answers."

"That's a good idea," Maggie said.

"I'm afraid I won't be able to be too hands-on, though," Maura said. "I'm working on training two new volunteers on our computer system."

"I know you're low on staff, so I'm sure they'll be a big help."

"I certainly hope so, although I've been thrown for a loop

already. My teenage niece is visiting for the summer and I expected her to pick it up like a charm. Wrong. She'll be the first to tell you that, frankly, she and computers do not get along. But would you believe it? I've got a seventysomething retiree who is an absolute whiz when it comes to technology."

"I guess you can't judge a book by its cover," Maggie said with a smile.

"On the nose, Maggie. Anyway, feel free to stop by later and I can at least get you started."

Maggie thanked her and wished her luck with training, then hung up. As she put her phone away, she glanced at the veil and groaned. She had forgotten to ask Maura to help her think of the book she was trying to remember. *I'll ask her when I stop by the library later.*

First, however, she thought she'd go over to Carriage House Antiques. June was always up for a good brainstorming session. She also could appraise items with the best in the business. If anyone could give Maggie strong counsel about how to research this designer Roaring Twenties wedding dress, it would be June.

As Maggie headed out the side door toward the antiques shop, dress in hand, Snickers slipped through too, apparently intent on following the fringe he found so enticing. After a short walk along a picturesque path, complete with a bridge over a small brook, they approached the quaint, nineteenth-century building that had once harbored horses and carriages but was now home to Carriage House Antiques. Distracted by a butterfly, Snickers scampered away in search of different prey.

Laughing at his antics, Maggie waved to June, who was just unlocking the front door and securing it open with an antique cast-iron doorstop in the shape of a Boston terrier.

"Maybe that dog door stopper is what sent Snickers off into

the bushes," Maggie said. "I think he just pretended interest in the butterfly."

"Nah, Snickers is made of stronger stuff than that. He was in full hunting mode," June said with a grin. "The weather is so beautiful today I figured we could air out the shop a little."

"Your parents were right to name you June," Maggie said. "This month is so bright and cheery, just like you."

"Why thank you," June said, leading the way back into the shop. "What's got you in such a good mood today?"

Maggie held up the dress in her arms. "I just found this amazing wedding dress in a closet."

June's grin widened. "Wow, what a gown. Are you trying to tell me something?"

Maggie laughed and hung the hanger on a wall hook. She frowned. "Oh no."

"What's wrong?" June asked.

"There was a veil too, but it's missing." Maggie peeked out the front door and looked toward the manor. "I don't see it along the path. It must have fallen off inside before I left. What if it gets more damaged?"

"Well, now I am thoroughly intrigued," June said. "Tell me everything."

Maggie relayed the story about how she had discovered the dress, leaving out the part where she had tried it on. *No need to stir up the rumor mill.* She quickly got to the point of why she'd brought it over in the first place. "I was hoping you might have an idea about why Aunt Evelyn would have had it, or at least something about its style and maker."

June examined the dress. "I worked for your aunt for many years, but Evelyn never mentioned this dress to me. It's not likely it was hers, of course. First of all, it doesn't appear to have been worn. And this style—it's called a 'chemise'—predates her courting period years by decades." June fiddled with the zipper. "It does seem to be authentically flapper, based on its mechanics. This zipper was actually called a 'separable fastener' back then."

"I actually don't know much about styles from that period," Maggie confessed.

"A lot of fashion reflected the social liberation women were experiencing because of the work they'd done during World War I," June said. "They had gained the right to vote, so suffrage was at its height. That generation redefined what women were supposed to be." She put air quotes around the word *supposed*. "More of them worked outside the home. The wild ones, called 'flappers,' smoked and danced and did other things that previous generations had considered unladylike. The shorter flapper dresses allowed women more comfort and freedom. See how it's straight and has no waist? That allowed women to abandon their corsets and move about more easily. It would have been hard to drive a car in a corset and petticoats, you know," she added with a wink.

"This is the first flapper-style wedding dress I've seen, that's for sure," Maggie said. "I always picture women wearing more-colorful versions for dancing the Charleston."

"Complete with feathered headband, satin gloves, and long pearls." June struck a pose, then both women burst out laughing. "After all their hard work in the factories in World War I, it's no surprise women wanted more comfortable clothing so they could live it up. But comfort doesn't have to mean boring by any small stretch of the imagination."

"Certainly not, if this dress is any indication." Maggie smoothed out the neckline, then brushed her fingertips across the label. "Do you know anything about the designer?"

"I know Jean Patierre was a Parisian designer in the early 1900s, but I don't know if he was still working after World War I.

Let's see if we can find out more."

The two women headed for the shop's computer. They searched online for a lead on the dressmaker but didn't find any information that indicated he'd designed flapper dresses, or even that he was still working in the 1920s. And they didn't find a single clue that could tell them how a stunning wedding dress by a French designer had ended up in a spare closet in small-town Maine.

"Well, that was a dead end," Maggie said. "I guess I'll keep searching for local history that could tell me more about it."

June sighed and fiddled with the cloisonné ballpoint pen around her neck. "I'll do more research too. Even without hard proof, though, I feel pretty confident in telling you that this dress is worth a fortune, Maggie."

"You think so?"

"It certainly has value, whether monetary, personal, or both."

Maggie gently ran her finger along the delicate beading on the neckline. "It's such a shame that it was hidden away for all those years."

June smiled brightly. "Well then, let's hide it no longer. I was just about to change out the display in the front window, and I've been toying with the idea of doing a wedding theme. This would be the perfect centerpiece. You can show off the dress while we work on researching its history, then decide on a more permanent solution later."

Maggie nodded in agreement. "It certainly would turn heads. What else should we include?"

"I can think of a few things." June darted around the store like a hummingbird, gathering merchandise. Soon she had collected a treasure trove of coordinating accessories, including faux pearl necklaces, a felt cloche hat trimmed with lace, soft fringed scarves, intricately beaded purses, and T-strap shoes, all of which were in varying shades of ivory and gold.

While June was clearing the old display out of the front window to make way for the wedding vignette, Maggie retrieved a mannequin from the workroom. With great care, she pulled the dress over it and zipped up the back, then set the mannequin right in front of the window.

"Time to accessorize this bride-to-be," June said. She looped pearl strands around the mannequin's neck, draped a coin purse strap across its hand, and set the cloche hat atop its head. She and Maggie worked together to move a couple of waist-high pillars into the space, which made perfect platforms for the T-strap shoes and a silver-plated vanity set.

"I have to hand it to you, June," Maggie said. "You can create window magic in a matter of minutes."

"If only my magic extended to knowing exactly where this dress came from." June adjusted the last of the pearls over a mirror, then snapped her fingers. "I have an idea. Let's sponsor a contest. Whoever can determine the true origin of the dress—with authentic proof of its history—will win a gift certificate to Carriage House Antiques."

"June, you are nonstop with the ideas today," Maggie said. "Let's make a poster to advertise it."

Half an hour later, the two women had entry forms made and a contest flyer in place in the window. They printed off a couple of extra copies to hang up in their friends' businesses. June had also hand-lettered a sign that said *Not for Sale* in pretty script, and Maggie set it on a wood easel at the base of the mannequin.

Admiring the finished display, Maggie said, "Not bad for a morning's work."

June pointed out the window toward the parking lot. "And it's already drawing a crowd."

Several women were approaching the shop. Maggie

recognized them and smiled. Leading the group with her typical power walk was petite, white-haired Ina Linton, the town's most spirited septuagenarian. Ruth Harper, president of the Somerset Harbor Historical Society and walking encyclopedia about the area, followed her. Liz Young—whose husband, David, served as the pastor at Old Faith Chapel, and who was a counselor in her own right—was with them. Maggie wondered if her friends were coming from coffee at The Busy Bean, their friend Daisy Carter's nearby café. If so, they'd likely be full of town gossip.

Maggie and June went outside to greet their fellow historical society members. After exchanging hellos and remarking on the day's beautiful weather, the women immediately started oohing and aahing over the new window display, especially the dress.

Ina, who had been power walking in place, stopped and pulled a notepad and pencil out of her fanny pack. "What's this contest sign all about? Sounds like a news story to me."

"News story?" June asked.

Ina nodded. "Thaddeus Jablonsky seems to think I have a nose for news, so he has hired me as the temporary society columnist for *The Somerset Harbor Herald* while the current columnist—bless her heart—recovers from gallbladder surgery."

"That's exciting, Ina," Liz said. "You'll be great."

"I personally thought that my police scanner made me a perfect candidate for the crime desk, but Thad told me he didn't really want to shuffle things around that much. So society page it is. And I think I'll start with a blurb about this interesting dress that seems to have walked right out of history." Ina's eyes lit up. "That's a nice line—'walked right out of history.'" Ina scribbled on her pad, then looked back at Maggie. "So anyway, what's this contest business?"

"I found this dress in one of my closets," Maggie said while Ina took notes in shorthand. "It's got a designer label, but it appears to have never been worn. We're hoping someone around town knows something about why it would have been in Sedgwick Manor. Aunt Evelyn didn't mention it in her journal, and she never said anything to June either."

"It seems to be a unique creation, but typical of a wedding dress from the Roaring Twenties," June said. "We didn't find anything about it online, so we thought we'd offer an incentive for folks around town to help us solve the mystery. Whoever can authenticate the dress's origin and history will get a gift certificate to the store."

"But not the dress?" Ina asked, still jotting notes.

"No, not the dress," Maggie said. "We may not know its history or value, but Aunt Evelyn must have thought it was important to have kept it. Maybe it has ties to my family, in which case I don't think I could part with it. Besides, maybe Emily would want to wear it for her own wedding someday. Or maybe I'd wear it to a costume party or something."

"Or you might wear it for its intended purpose, perhaps?" Ina looked up, eyes sparkling, pencil poised for an answer.

Maggie laughed. "I have no need for a wedding dress, if that's what you want to know, Ina."

Ina gave a woebegone sigh. "I thought I had a real scoop for the society column for a moment there."

She turned toward the window and jotted down the details of the contest from the poster as Ruth and Liz complimented June on the stylistic details of the display.

Over the murmur of conversation, Maggie heard something akin to a bicycle bell ringing. She and the other ladies turned to see a two-wheeled, self-balancing vehicle zipping down the driveway toward the antiques shop. Maggie had seen mall security officers riding similar vehicles, but she'd never expected to see one in quiet Somerset Harbor.

A tall figure wearing a helmet with a lightning bolt decal was at the helm of the Segway, ringing a bell attached to the steering column. As the vehicle came to a stop, they could see it was piloted by a tall older woman, who peered at them from beneath the helmet.

Maggie stepped in front of the others. "Hello?"

The woman, clad in black leather from head to toe, stepped off the vehicle and put down the kickstand, then undid her chin strap and removed the helmet. To Maggie's surprise, the woman's hair was dyed flame-red and cut in a no-nonsense bob. Adopting a military stance, she asked, "Can I interest anyone in a tour of Somerset Harbor?"

Maggie, Ruth, Liz, and Ina gaped at her.

The woman stuck out her right hand toward Maggie. "Maxine MacDonald."

Maggie shook her hand. "Maggie Watson." She introduced the others, then asked, "Was that a joke, your comment about the tour?"

"No ma'am," Maxine said, reaching into her jacket pocket. "Here's my card. Lean On Me Tour Company." She passed out her business cards, which had a photo of her riding a patroller on a mountain trail. "I rent out Segways, which are a great way to tour an area. You can cover a lot of ground quickly, but not so fast that you miss things."

"We all live here, but it would certainly be an interesting way to see our town." Ina flipped her notepad to a new page. "So, tell us about your new business, Maxine."

"I was in the army for decades," Maxine said. "Served in the military police corps. After retirement, I worked mall security in Boston. Last year, I decided to escape the big city for a quieter life in Somerset Harbor. But then it seemed a little too quiet, at least for me.

So I started my personal vehicle business. I do tours and sales."

"You know, the Somerset Harbor Police Department might find them valuable as replacements for its bicycles," Ruth said thoughtfully. "You should talk to Chief Rick Cole."

"These vehicles are ideal for law enforcement," Maxine said. "Thank you for the suggestion, ma'am." After a beat, she cleared her throat. "Anyone for a test drive?"

"You betcha." Ever the adventurer, Ina was the first to volunteer. The other ladies exchanged glances. Ina had never been seen driving a car and was notorious for walking everywhere in town, no matter the weather.

"But Ina, you don't drive," Liz said.

"So what?" Ina turned to Maxine. "That doesn't mean I can't ride one of these contraptions, right?"

"All you need are two feet, two hands, and a sense of adventure," Maxine said. "Let me show you how it works."

The women all watched intently as Maxine did a short demo right in front of the shop. "Lean in the direction you want to go," she said. "It's all balance and movement." She explained that the vehicle would adjust with the rider's lean, moving and steadying to keep the rider upright. "Of course, you have to use your brain too. Don't drive into a tree, for goodness' sake."

"Ina, are you sure you want to do this?" Maggie asked. Ina might have the vigor of a woman half her age, but Maggie still wondered if this was a good idea.

"It's a glorified scooter, dear," Ina said. "I'll just take it down the lane a bit and circle right back."

After Ina got the helmet on, Maxine folded up the kickstand and pushed the power button. "You're in balance mode—just lean the way you want to go. Lean forward if you want to go forward, lean back if you want to go back, and lean to the side if you want to turn."

Ina stepped on and wobbled, which the vehicle magnified. "Whoa!" It took her a few nerve-rattling seconds, but she got it under control.

"Hold right there. Let me get a picture of this for my website," Maxine said, snapping photos with her phone as Ina continued to balance on the transporter. "Hope you don't mind if I blitz the Internet with this pic."

"Sure, sure, but wrap it up. I'm ready to take this thing for a spin."

Maxine nodded and put her phone away. Ina hooted with glee as she and the vehicle took off down the driveway.

"Not to worry, ladies," Maxine said, apparently noticing the apprehension on their faces. "She'll figure it out. Now what do we have here?" Maxine strode toward the shop window, took a swift look at the wedding display, and headed for the front door.

Maggie followed Maxine inside while Ruth, Liz, and June watched after Ina. Maxine got out her cell phone again and began taking pictures of the dress, then peppered Maggie with a litany of pointed questions.

"Where and how did you get the dress? Whose was it? What event did the owner wear it to? When did you get it? Who is the maker of the dress? Was there a designer? Was it handmade?"

As she answered "I don't know" to almost every question, Maggie started to feel as though she were being interrogated by the former MP.

Seemingly out of questions, Maxine ran her hands over the gown, admiring the fabric and details. Then she started to unzip the dress. "I want to try it on."

"I'm sorry, no," Maggie said. "It's not for sale. See the sign?"

"It's in this shop, isn't it? I'll take it as is." Maxine continued to move the zipper down.

Maggie stepped between Maxine and the dress. "Ms. MacDonald, it's nice to have you in our community, and while we would certainly appreciate your business here in Carriage House Antiques, the dress is not for sale. It's something connected to my family, and—"

Maxine put her index finger up close to Maggie's face. "Let me tell *you* something." She began raising her voice. "I believe it is connected to *my* family. Look at this." She pulled her wallet out of her pants pocket and held up a photo cut out of a newspaper that depicted a woman wearing a white dress. The clipping had been laminated, but the creased and yellowed paper showed clear signs of age.

Maggie couldn't believe the similarity. "The dresses do look alike—but how could that be?"

June, who must have heard their discussion through the open door, appeared next to Maggie. "Is there a question you have that I can help you with, Maxine?"

Maxine put the photo away into her wallet. "No, nothing. Just asking about this contest you have advertised here."

Maggie raised her eyebrows but didn't contradict Maxine. If the dress was somehow connected to the older woman's family, Maggie could certainly understand her emotions.

June handed Maxine one of the contest flyers. "The contest will end one week from today. No one can win the dress—it's Maggie's. We are just looking for information about it. But you could win a nice gift certificate to our shop."

Just then, they heard a voice from outside. "Help! Maggie, June, help!"

3

The cries were getting louder by the moment. Maggie, June, and Maxine ran outside. Ina zoomed toward the shop, shouting, "How do I stop this thing?"

Maxine came to a halt and stood up straight with her hands in the air. "Stand up," she commanded.

"What?" Ina tilted her head in confusion to the left, and the vehicle veered in the same direction—and right toward Snickers, who was strolling back toward the manor.

Snickers was carefully stalking a squirrel and apparently hadn't noticed Ina approaching from behind him. Maggie gasped. "Snickers!"

Immediately, Ina leaned back, sending the vehicle abruptly in reverse. She and the transporter toppled onto the grass, just feet away from where Liz and Ruth were watching, eyes wide.

Maggie ran to Ina but stopped at her side, unsure if she should move her. Ina sat for a moment, legs sprawled out in front of her, patting herself as though she were checking to see if all parts were in the right places. Then she made as if to stand.

Maggie helped Ina to her feet. "Are you all right, Ina? That was quite a spill."

"All right?" Ina laughed. "I'm fantastic. At my age, thrills like that are hard to come by."

"Do you think you should rest a minute?" Ruth asked.

"Need a glass of water?" June offered.

"Do you want a ride home?" Maggie volunteered.

Ina waved them all off. "No time to waste," she said. "I've got a story to write and then some. Best get home." With a dismissive salute, she tromped down the lane toward town.

"That woman never ceases to amaze," Ruth said. "Now she's writing news stories for the paper? I don't know where she finds the energy for everything."

"Or the time," Liz said. "She also volunteered to help coordinate the Old Faith tag sale next month."

"Speaking of which," June said, "Maggie and I set aside some items to donate. Do you want to come look at them?"

"Yes, please," Liz said. "And thank you. What a huge help."

As the ladies headed into the shop, Maggie noticed that Maxine was inspecting the Segway, which seemed quite all right to Maggie. "Is there anything I can do?"

"Yes indeed. You can sell me that dress if you want to make up for this disaster—encouraging that crazy woman to drive my vehicle."

"But I—" Maggie was not about to take responsibility for Ina's accident or Maxine's misjudgment in letting a total beginner ride the patroller without a chaperone.

"You'll be hearing from me." Maxine stepped onto her Segway, and Maggie heard her mutter something indistinct as she drove away.

A shiver went through Maggie. She stood there for a few moments, rubbing her crossed arms in spite of the day's warmth. Maxine's attitude had made her feel very uncomfortable—asking all those questions and intimidating her with misguided blame for Ina's spill.

Maggie sat down on a wrought-iron bench in front of the shop. Snickers jumped into her lap. "Glad to see you escaped unharmed, buddy," she said, scratching his ears gently. "What do you think about all this?"

The cat purred under her hand until there was a rustle in a nearby tree. The squirrel had returned, and Snickers took off to once again protect the property from intruders. *There goes my four-legged security system.*

As Maggie stood to walk back into the shop, she noticed something sparkling on the path that led from the manor to the carriage house, right about the spot where Ina had taken her tumble. She bent down and picked up what appeared to be a diamond engagement ring. As she inspected the sparkling stone and its setting of intricate white gold flourishes, she wondered where it had come from. *Could it be Ina's?* That was a silly idea. Ina had never married. What would she be doing with a diamond engagement ring?

Could it be Maxine's? Equally silly—although the woman had seemed quite desperate to purchase the wedding dress.

Maggie walked into the shop and joined Liz, Ruth, and June, who were gathered around a pine dough table the shop was donating to the tag sale.

"Maggie, the items you're giving us are just wonderful," Liz said. "Thank you so much. I'm going to go tell David all about them now."

"You're so welcome, Liz. We're always glad to help."

"I'd better get going too," Ruth said. "We have a school group coming by the historical society museum later today and I need to prepare. Though there's no way to fully prepare for twenty fifth graders."

"Before you go, did anyone lose a ring?" Maggie held out her hand to show them the engagement ring. "I found it on the ground just now."

Liz examined the ring. "No, but it sure is pretty."

June shook her head. "It's not from the shop."

"It looks vintage to me," Ruth said. "Sorry, that's all the help I can be."

"No problem. It was great seeing you ladies this morning." Maggie walked them to the door and said goodbye. As she caught a glimpse of the wedding display in the front window, Maggie had a thought. *What if the ring had been with the dress—perhaps in a pocket?*

She approached the display and felt the left side of the dress. Yes, there was a pocket there. She put her hand inside. It was large enough to hold a ring, and it was deep enough for the ring to have sat there securely for quite some time. The pocket was empty. Then she felt on the right side of the dress. Another pocket. She slipped her hand in, and all the way down at the bottom she felt something. She pulled it out. A wedding ring.

She put the two rings together. They were a perfect fit.

Wanting to see the jewelry better, Maggie walked out the front door and held them in the bright sunlight. As she examined the rings, a classic 1950s tan-and-brown Chevrolet sedan pulled up to the shop with a squeal of brakes on the tires. The door opened and out came a woman who looked as though she had stepped off the pages of a 1950s fashion magazine.

Lowering her cat-eye sunglasses onto the bridge of her nose and peering down at Maggie, she said, "Missy, I have a bone to pick with you."

Maggie sighed. *Now what?* She assessed the commanding figure in front of her.

With her flawless makeup and dyed-blonde pixie haircut, the woman in a light blue shift and matching cardigan could have been any age, although Maggie spied a few age spots on the backs of her hands. Thanks to light blue heels that matched her dress, the woman towered over Maggie. She pulled a vintage handkerchief from her vinyl handbag and snapped the purse shut, then removed her sunglasses and used the handkerchief to clean them. When she looked up again, her gaze pierced through Maggie.

"Did you see that?" The woman gestured toward the trees beyond the manor.

Maggie looked in the direction the woman was pointing, placing the rings in her pocket as she stood. "No, I am afraid I didn't see anything. What happened?"

"I was turning into your lane here when a crazy woman on a mall cop scooter came out of nowhere and ran me off the road. Off the road, I say! Even if you had a stop sign there, as you should, I'm sure that nut would have blown right through it. I had to swerve into the ditch, and it took me ages to extricate Beulah from its depths."

"Beulah?" Maggie looked around. She didn't see anyone else.

The woman stroked the driver's-side fender of her car. "Beulah is my ever-faithful companion on the roadway of life."

Maggie blinked several times. She was well practiced in revering the classic Chevrolet Bel Air. Her grandfather would take her out on special occasions in his aqua Bel Air station wagon, driving smoothly along Vermont's windy roads. At just the right time they would pull off by the side of the road, put down the tailgate, and eat apple slices and egg salad sandwiches wrapped in waxed paper. People who still had '57 Chevys in mint condition would be inclined to be protective of them. And the woman in front of her obviously had a flair for anything vintage.

However, as Maggie looked over the car, there seemed to be nothing scratched or dented, only a bit of mud and grass on the tires. Maggie could only imagine what her lawn might look like.

"I'm certainly sorry for your trouble." Maggie realized that they had not introduced themselves. *Maybe that will soothe the savage motorist.* "I'm Maggie Watson. This is my shop, Carriage House Antiques."

The woman patted her brow with the handkerchief. "Harriet Hamstead. I'm the proprietor of the new vintage clothing shop downtown, A Fine Vintage. I thought I'd come to introduce myself, since we both must appreciate the past. I had heard that your shop primarily focused on furnishings, and I thought you might have some furniture pieces that I could use for fixtures in the store. My vintage pieces should not be displayed with modern furniture. It would look ridiculous. But I'm just so upset. I could have been run off the cliff."

Maggie winced. Harriet obviously had a flair for the dramatic. The driveway entrance to the antiques shop was hardly near the cliff.

She edged toward the front door of the shop. "Harriet, I would love for you to see the store. And I'd like to introduce you to June, my manager. I'm sure she can help you find what you're looking for at a price you find agreeable."

Maggie could see that Harriet had calmed down some but was still of a mind to make the most of her troubles.

Harriet started following Maggie into the shop, then halted next to the display window. "Oh my goodness. What is this beautiful creation you have here? A flapper dress in a creamy white? It's perfection. I must have it to complete my collection."

Maggie sighed. *Here we go again.*

For the umpteenth time that day, Maggie explained just about everything she knew about the dress. "Everybody loves it, Harriet, but I am sorry to tell you that it is not for sale. See the sign right here next to the dress? It's special to me—something of my aunt's that I plan to keep."

Harriet did a bit of harrumphing and then resorted to some sniffing as well, although Maggie was certain she saw no actual tears. "I just keep flashing back to my near-death experience moments ago," Harriet said, her voice equal parts weepy and haughty. "If your driveway was properly marked, I might not have been so endangered. I might be willing to forget what just happened if you let me purchase this little number. A wise businesswoman would want to keep her customer happy in a situation like this." She shook her head haughtily. "You see, as a shop owner myself, I know what it takes to please my clientele. A Fine Vintage specializes in vintage dresses and formalwear. I've spent years putting together a museum-quality display of wedding gowns from each decade of the twentieth century. It will be my main attraction."

Maggie nodded politely but was still resolved not to budge on her decision to keep the dress.

"Many young — and older — women have themed weddings," Harriet continued with a note of authority. "The '50s, the '60s, and so on. I have wedding dresses from all the decades of the twentieth century except the 1920s, the flapper period. This would complete my collection for my big opening day. I am blitzing this all over the Internet, you know. In a week, Somerset Harbor will be buzzing with brides-to-be and bridesmaids-to-be and mothers-of-the-bride-to-be and — well, you get the picture."

Maggie gulped. She had indeed. Then something clicked — hadn't someone else that morning said something about sharing something all over the Internet? First Maxine MacDonald and now Harriet Hamstead. *Whatever draws in customers is good for the whole town, I suppose.*

"Harriet, why don't we go inside and you can meet June. She's a whiz when it comes to antique and vintage furniture, and I'm sure she'll help you find something you like."

"I drove all the way here. I might as well do what I came for."

Harriet followed Maggie into the shop, where they found June at the front counter.

"June, this is Harriet Hamstead," Maggie said. "She's opening up that new vintage clothing shop, A Fine Vintage."

"How wonderful to meet you," June said. "I know everyone in town is excited about your opening day reception, Harriet. And if you love antique clothing, you should consider coming to one of our historical society meetings to share your knowledge with us. I'm sure the other members would love to learn from you."

Maggie could sense a shift in Harriet's prickly demeanor as June's effervescent personality won her over. "June, Harriet stopped by because she's interested in antique furniture that could serve as fixtures in her store. Can you think of anything we have that might work for her?"

"I'm sure I can," June said. "Come with me, Harriet. Tell me more about your shop and your vision."

Harriet started up an enthusiastic description of her business as she and June walked off to tour the shop.

Glad to see that Harriet's mood had shifted, Maggie breathed a sigh of relief. Her mind shifted back to the mysterious rings, and she slipped her hand into her jeans pocket. As her fingers wrapped around the rings, she wondered if Aunt Evelyn's journal made any mention of an engagement-wedding ring set.

She scribbled a note for June letting her know she'd gone back to Sedgwick Manor, then headed back up the path. She smiled when Snickers joined her. "Had enough squirrel chasing for one day?"

As Maggie entered the side door, she winced when she saw the torn veil lying in a crumpled heap on the floor. "At least it didn't fall off in the mud outside," she said to Snickers, who was trotting toward his food dish and paid her no mind. She carefully picked up the veil, smoothed out the tulle, and carried it to the master suite.

Remembering Snickers's antics from earlier, she draped the veil over some folded sweaters on the top shelf of her closet. It was as safe a place as any. *Now, to do some digging in Aunt Evelyn's journal.*

In the library, Maggie sat down at the desk and found Evelyn's antiques journal in the top drawer. She rubbed the smooth brown leather, remembering her aunt fondly—her feisty personality, her diminutive frame, her sharp blue eyes that radiated warmth and energy behind her wire-rimmed glasses, her love for gatherings with friends and for sharing bits of wisdom.

Maggie pulled the rings out of her jeans pocket and set them in front of her. Then, page by page, she looked through the journal for any mention of rings. About a third of the way through the book, Maggie found an entry dated about a decade earlier. *One lot of ten rings of various types and styles from Jonathan Smith Estate farm auction. Four gold, six silver.*

Maggie looked at the set of rings on the desk. She knew the rings were white gold, but they could have been initially mistaken for silver. *Probably not by Aunt Evelyn, though.* There was no mention of a matching pair. Besides, why would these rings have been in the pocket of the wedding dress if they had been part of a lot purchased at auction for the shop?

Maggie booted up the computer and did an Internet search on 1920s wedding rings. Hundreds of images appeared on the screen, and she scrolled through them slowly, studying the designs. White gold was apparently common for that time. The swirly pattern on the engagement ring she'd found that morning appeared repeatedly in the photos, and Maggie read that it was called a fleur-de-lis design. *The flower of the lily traditionally represents the ideals of perfection, light, and life,* the site stated.

Maggie reached for her reading glasses and studied the intricate design of the engagement ring more closely. She squinted as something on the inside of the band caught her eye. It was an inscription.

E & J.

That was all.

So who was the *E*? Evelyn? Not likely, Maggie thought, since her uncle's name had been George.

Maggie sighed as she realized she was at a dead end. She grabbed the rings, got up from the desk, and walked to the master suite. She picked up the wooden musical jewelry box her late husband, Richard, had given her as a wedding gift. When she opened it, Beethoven's "Ode to Joy" played. The theme always reminded her to find joy in the moment and to be thankful for all situations. She placed the rings in the box—they would be safe there. But now what?

Maggie wanted to meet with Maura at the library—she might have some ideas or could at least point her in the right direction.

Another idea was to look in the archives at *The Somerset Harbor Herald*. Perhaps an old issue of the newspaper had a wedding announcement that fit the clues she had discovered. Sedgwick Manor and its inhabitants had always been integral to the community, so anything related to the family would have gotten top billing on the society page.

She could also ask Ruth for help searching through the repository of marriage licenses, letters, and other artifacts relating to local history at the Somerset Harbor Historical Society Museum. A couple of hours poring through files there could help her locate information leading to the rightful owner of the wedding dress, veil, and rings.

Maggie's thoughts were interrupted by the ring of her cell phone. She pulled the phone out of her jeans pocket and answered it.

"Hi, June."

"Maggie, I know the morning has been a bit crazy, but something else has come up."

Maggie sensed concern in June's voice. "What's going on?"

"Harriet—you know, the lady who was here—is still insistent on having the flapper wedding dress. She says that if we don't give it to her, she could sue us for damage to property, negligence, harassment, and mental stress."

Maggie's eyes widened. "I'm so sorry, June. Everything seemed fine when I left."

"I thought it was too. I showed her around the shop and pointed out some things she might want, like those French Provincial chairs we got last month. She seemed happy, but then she saw the dress again on the way out and got very . . . snippy."

"What did you tell her?"

"I told her we'd have to talk about it before giving her an answer. It was the only thing I could think of."

"That's fine, June. We'll find a way to calm her down."

The ladies chatted a bit longer about shop business, then said goodbye. Maggie took a deep breath. *If this dress is such a coveted item, I'd better get to work figuring out who it belongs to. Before someone decides it belongs to them and just takes it.*

4

A text from her friend James Bennett shook Maggie out of her unpleasant musings. *Busy as a bean?*

She knew what that meant: "Let's meet up at The Busy Bean." It was now well past lunchtime, and the café's signature club sandwich and homemade potato chips were calling her name. After grabbing her purse and checking her hair in the foyer mirror, Maggie headed toward town.

A few minutes' walk later, Maggie caught sight of The Busy Bean's cheerful yellow-and-white striped canopy. She smiled at the sign, which depicted a bee dive-bombing a cup of coffee.

As Maggie walked through the front door, she was pleased to see that James had already secured his usual table next to the window. She waved to him, then held up a single finger indicating she'd be over in a minute. First, she wanted to say hello to Daisy Carter, her good friend and the café's owner.

Dressed in a bold-patterned blouse and wearing a wide pink headband around her brunette beehive, the former pageant queen was easy to find at the register. "Hi, Daisy," Maggie said as she approached.

"Hey, sweetie," Daisy said in her trademark Southern drawl. She had moved from Georgia to Somerset Harbor decades earlier after winning the restaurant in an essay contest, but she had never lost her accent. "Having lunch with James, are we?" She raised a perfectly shaped eyebrow.

Always with an ear for gossip, Daisy had a knack for making a perfectly innocent lunch date sound much more important than it was. Shifting focus, Maggie held out a flyer for the wedding dress contest. "Daisy, would you consider posting this in your window?"

Taking the flyer and skimming it, Daisy said, "You don't even have to ask. I'll find a spot for it where everybody can see it."

Maggie thanked Daisy and headed for James's table. However, as she turned in that direction, she realized that someone else had his attention. Somerset Harbor's recently deputized society reporter was standing at James's table with her notepad and pencil at the ready.

"Hello, you two," Maggie said brightly as she approached. "Did you find another source for your column, Ina?"

"I was just getting James's reaction to the wedding dress contest." Ina jotted down a few notes. "I started working up my column inches and realized that I was short one or two, so I thought I'd see what the most eligible bachelor in town might think of such a thing."

James, trying and failing to hide a grin, cleared his throat. "I don't know that I'm the *most* eligible bachelor in town, Ina."

Maggie settled into a turquoise vinyl chair across from James. With a smirk, she asked, "Well, as *one of* the most eligible bachelors in town, what do you think of the contest?"

"As a businessman, I think it's a great way to drum up traffic to your shop. And as an alderman, I think you'll spark interest in the town's history, which I am always on board with."

"Are you catching all this, Ina?" Maggie tried to peek at the notes scribbled on Ina's pad.

"Of course I am. I've known shorthand for years. Now, if you'll excuse me, I've got somewhere to be."

James chuckled as he watched Ina stride out of the café. "I wonder if Thad knew what he was getting himself into when he hired Ina for the society page."

Maggie chuckled. "One way or another, it'll be a fun read."

She glanced at the menu. "What sounds good?"

"Maggie, you know you don't even need to look at that menu." He took it from her hands and laid it on the table. "Let me guess—a club sandwich with homemade potato chips."

Maggie looked at him expectantly. "And?"

"And—" he peered at her face "—you look like you need the house blend today. But only if it's strong."

"Bingo." She grabbed his menu and set it down on the table along with hers. "Venturing a guess, you'll have an egg sandwich and a piece of apple pie."

Jenny, the waitress, stopped by to take their order and brought back mugs of coffee just a minute later.

Hands cupped around her mug, Maggie said, "So, what's new in Somerset Harbor, Mr. Alderman?"

James took a sip of coffee, then set down his cup. "As a matter of fact, things are zipping along, figuratively and literally. Have you seen an interesting woman running around town on one of those battery-powered scooters you stand on?"

"Maxine MacDonald? I met her today."

"I've been getting a lot of calls from citizens and other council members about her," James said. "She chased someone's dog down the street last week. She was seen cutting corners over Ruby Adams's front lawn, leaving two parallel lines that are not bouncing back well, according to Ruby. And she seems to think she's the unofficial crossing guard at the school. She even stops traffic over there when she sees fit."

Maggie nodded sympathetically. "Did any of those folks call the police?"

"Yes," James said, then lowered his voice. "But Chief Cole called me and asked me to deal with Ms. MacDonald in a quiet manner. It seems she's former military police, and he doesn't feel right chastising one of his own for what he calls trivial matters."

"And have you talked to her?"

"Sure I have," James said. "First, there was the matter of a lack of a business license, so we got her squared away with that. She's selling those mall cop things, you know."

"Segways."

"Yes, those."

Jenny appeared to deliver their lunch, then refilled their coffee and headed back to the kitchen.

Maggie savored a chip. "Maxine told me she's offering tours. I'm afraid I don't see her as the tour guide type, especially since she hasn't been in town all that long. I'm sure she couldn't give as thorough a tour as Ruth or Ina."

"She's got half a dozen of the vehicles to rent, and customers would be allowed to take them out without her," James said. "She lives next to my friend Everett, and she works out of her garage. She even created a stylized map of Somerset Harbor and the area with various historical landmarks noted. It's quite nice, actually."

"Does she demonstrate how to operate the things first?" Maggie asked, unable to keep the bitterness out of her voice. "When she visited the antiques shop this morning, she barely gave Ina any instruction before letting her drive off. Poor Ina crash-landed on her way back."

"But Ina doesn't drive," James said, taking a bite of his egg sandwich.

"I know," Maggie said. "Maxine insisted she didn't need to. I think she should check to see if someone has a driver's license first, don't you?"

"I'm not sure. And that's part of the problem. She just sort of jumped in with these business ventures without going through all the permitting processes. That's partly how I got involved. We'll get it all figured out." James stole one of Maggie's chips. "So, you got to know her a bit today?"

Maggie explained how Maxine had been rather aggressive at the shop, demanding she sell the wedding dress in the window.

"Is this the famous dress that inspired your contest?"

"Let me start at the beginning," Maggie said, then gave him the entire story of her morning.

"So what's the big deal?" he asked. "Not your normal wedding gown, I'm guessing."

"Not quite." Maggie showed him the photo she had taken earlier of herself wearing the gown, hoping the heat rushing to her face would go unnoticed.

"I'm not an expert on fashion," James said, "but I agree that it is quite a remarkable dress. It could just be the lady wearing it, of course." He grinned at her.

Trying to ignore that her face was probably the same shade as a boiled lobster, Maggie continued with her story, including the engagement and wedding rings she had also found. "You knew my aunt Evelyn a long time, James. Did she ever mention a romance connected with Sedgwick Manor or my family? A couple with the initials *E* and *J*?"

James paused for a moment. "I remember some sort of story about a wedding that was supposed to take place—not hers but a relative's. But it didn't happen. Some sort of tragedy or falling out. I don't think Evelyn told me directly. You know how people tell tales around here, so it may or may not be true. It's possible there's something in the *Herald* archives about it."

Maggie's eyes lit up. "If there was a falling out, maybe that explains the torn veil."

"Torn veil?"

Maggie leaned toward James. "I also found a veil with the dress—in fabric and design that matched perfectly. But it was torn from the bottom to the top."

"Just like in *Jane Eyre*."

"*Jane Eyre.*" Maggie sat back. "That's the name of the novel I was trying to remember. Remind me what happens in it."

"It's a classic by Charlotte Brontë. I don't remember it all that well because I read it for my high school English class. Jane, a governess, becomes engaged to her employer, Edward Rochester, but as their wedding plans are coming together, Jane finds her wedding veil ripped from the bottom to the top."

"Who would do that? Do they live happily ever after?" Maggie said.

James took a sip of coffee. "You have to read the book to find out. Let me just suggest, Maggie, that maybe you ought to check your attic."

"For?"

"That's all I'm going to say right now," James said with a wink. "It would certainly be a coincidence if the story of your dress is anything like that of *Jane Eyre*. But you should go check that book out at the library."

"Actually, the library is my next stop. When I talked to her earlier, Maura mentioned something about the Brontë sisters too."

At that moment, the front door of the café flew open with a bang and Harriet Hamstead strode right up to the front counter with an air of purpose about her.

Oh no. Maggie looked down, wondering if she could avoid a confrontation. She heard Harriet introducing herself first to Daisy, then Jenny, then the other customers at the counter. A moment later, she heard the *clip-clip* of Harriet's high heels getting closer. Maggie glanced up.

"Hello. Harriet Hamstead, A Fine Vintage," Harriet said, holding out her right hand and then retracting it. "Why, if it isn't the woman who owes me a wedding dress. What a coincidence."

Harriet turned toward James and handed him a business card. "And you are?"

"James Bennett," he said, setting the card on the table and then extending his hand toward her.

"I hear you're the mayor," Harriet said, shaking his hand.

"Alderman, actually," he said. "Nice to meet you. Good to have you here in Somerset Harbor. I've heard wonderful things about the shop you plan to open. I'm not much of an expert in vintage clothing, but I do have an interest in history and restoration."

Harriet began to explain some of the kinds of clothing she was going to sell in her store. While they were talking, Maggie examined the teal business card on the table. It featured a black-and-white photo of Harriet wearing a 1950s dress with pearls. Across the top it read, *A Fine Vintage: Everything Is Better With Age.*

Maggie slowly looked up at Harriet. If she wasn't mistaken, the woman seemed quite drawn to James. In fact, Harriet was now pulling over a chair to sit down at the end of the table.

Not wanting to be rude but feeling the need to get on with her day, Maggie said, "I'm sorry, but will you both excuse me?"

"Yeah, yeah," Harriet said, making a dismissive gesture with her hand.

Maggie pulled some money out of her wallet and set it on the table for her lunch, then stood and walked to the exit. Just as she opened the door, she found herself face to face with Maxine MacDonald, wearing black leather and a scowl.

"Maggie Watson, was it you who called the police on me?"

5

Maggie's eyes quickly went to Harriet, who was still talking to James near the window. If Harriet caught sight of Maxine, there could be trouble. Maggie decided to feign ignorance. "What do you mean?"

"Someone called the cops on me—said I nearly ran her over or something like that near your store."

"That's terrible."

"You're telling me. It just seems like people in this town have it out for me. I thought bringing in a new business would wake it up a bit, add a little fun for the tourists. And I try to help out around town—like with traffic at the school crossing and when the fire trucks go out—but all I get in response is complaints." Maxine shook her head and looked at the floor.

Maggie felt a rush of sympathy for Maxine. Despite all her bluster, maybe she was just trying to find a way to fit into their small town. Maggie knew all too well how hard it could be, moving to Somerset Harbor as an adult, trying to make friends with folks who had known each other all their lives. And the former MP standing in front of her holding a helmet with a lightning bolt certainly wasn't the most diplomatic person Maggie had ever met. Taking and giving orders in the army was probably the only lifestyle Maxine knew. She barked at people because she had been barked at most of her adult life. She probably assumed responsibilities that hadn't been asked of her because she had taken command of challenging situations in the military police. Maybe Maxine just needed a friend.

"Maxine, have you been to our library yet?" Maggie asked.

"I'm going over there right now. Would you like to join me?"
And if it prevents an altercation between Maxine and Harriet, so be it.

Maxine had a blank look on her face for a moment. Then
it changed to confusion. "Are you kidding me? Do I look like a
library kind of girl? I'm ready for action. I want to go and do, not
sit and read." With that she glanced around the room.

Maggie had a sinking feeling.

Maxine pointed toward James and Harriet. "Is that the crazy
lady who almost ran me over?" Her voice was loud enough for
everyone in The Busy Bean to hear, including James and Harriet,
who turned toward its source. And just like that, the former MP
was on the march.

Just then, Maggie's phone rang.

"Hello?"

"Maggie, hi. It's Maura O'Brien. Just wanted to let you know
that I had a few minutes this morning and I pulled some books
on 1920s fashion for you if you are still interested."

"How nice of you, thank you," Maggie said. "I know you're
busy, so I really appreciate it."

"It was no bother. I was in that section anyway. Are you
available to come by now?"

Maggie looked over at James's table, where it didn't appear
that World War III had started yet, so she told Maura she'd be right
over and left the café. James could fill her in later on whatever
happened between the feuding women.

The Somerset Harbor Public Library was a quick walk over
one block and up another. Soon Maggie was climbing the steps
to the library and opening the heavy front door.

Maura was at her front counter stool working on her desktop
computer, joined by two others who were also staring at her
screen. On Maura's left, an older woman was hunched over
in concentration. She had silvery-white hair in a long, single

braid down her back and was dressed in a long-sleeve black T-shirt with Edgar Allen Poe's face under the words *Once upon a midnight dreary.* Maggie thought she recognized her from somewhere, but figured she'd seen her in passing at the grocery store or on the street.

The other figure was a tall, slim girl of about seventeen whose dyed-black hair had bright pink tips. She wore a serious expression emphasized by her dark eyeshadow and a black top with cutouts that showed off her shoulders.

Maura looked up at Maggie over her reading glasses but kept her fingers on the keyboard. "That was a quick trip."

"I was just at The Busy Bean having lunch," Maggie said. "Thanks again for pulling books for me. Do you just want to point me in the right direction?"

"Sure, they're on a table in the back. First, let me introduce you to my newest volunteers." She gestured toward the older lady first. "This is Pearl Winters. She moved here last summer, to that neighborhood where Ina Linton lives—maybe you've seen her around town. She worked in the downtown Boston public library for nearly fifty years. She was its expert in all things computer and is going to help me get our card catalog online. That's not easy, you know."

"I can imagine," Maggie said, extending her hand to shake Pearl's. "Nice to meet you. I'm Maggie. I own Carriage House Antiques and live in the house next door."

Maura nodded. "She knows the difference between RAM and ROM."

"Well, that makes one of us," Maggie said.

Pearl's attention remained focused on the computer.

"She's a little shy," Maura said. "We librarians prefer the company of books to the company of people, don't we, Pearl?"

Pearl made a face. "Books aren't companions. They're paper and binding."

Maura laughed. "Well, not literally, no. But a good book never disappoints you. They help you feel connected to the characters in the story, so sometimes reading can be like making a new friend." She turned her attention to the younger girl. "And this is my niece, Mary Catherine Johnson."

"I prefer Magenta," the girl said quietly, shaking Maggie's hand.

"Matches your hair," Maggie said, smiling. "Nice to meet you, Magenta."

Maura explained that Mary Catherine—Magenta—was training to serve as an intern for the summer. "Time to get her nose out of a book and in front of a computer, which I'm sorry to say is not her forte. She's a bookworm like her auntie."

"Who's your favorite author, Magenta?" Maggie asked.

"Brontë," Magenta said almost immediately. "Anything Charlotte, Emily, or Anne. I've read *Wuthering Heights* like twelve times. I love Heathcliff."

"That's interesting. Just today a friend of mine recommended *Jane Eyre*. I assume you have a copy here, Maura?"

"We'd be a sorry excuse for a library if we didn't," Maura said. "Mary Catherine, could you please get it for Maggie?"

"Magenta," the girl muttered under her breath as she turned and stomped toward the fiction shelves in her black skinny jeans, studded black belt, and black combat boots.

"Oh, I can get it," Maggie said, hurrying after Magenta.

She caught up to the girl in the fiction section as she was examining a shelf marked *Bl–Bu*. Magenta located *Jane Eyre*, pulled a copy off the shelf, and handed it to Maggie.

"Thank you," Maggie said. She looked at the girl in front of her and thought of Emily, who was also living in a new town with few friends. Perhaps this sullen girl was lonely. "So, Magenta, are you enjoying your time in Somerset Harbor?"

Magenta shifted her feet and started straightening up books on the shelf. As she did, she answered. "Well, it's better than being home in Amherst. My parents are getting a divorce. Dad moved out six months ago, and Mom and I aren't getting along. She doesn't like my friends or the way I dress. I'd really like to go live with my dad in Vermont for the summer. We used to get along great, but he's got a girlfriend now, I guess, and I'd probably be in the way." Magenta kept straightening books.

"I'm sorry," Maggie said. "So, you're staying with your aunt this summer?"

"Yeah, it's okay. I'm getting my senior project hours done, and I'm learning things on the computer, and in my downtime I get to read."

Maggie watched how carefully Magenta lined up each book. Occasionally, she'd grab a book that must have been misshelved and place it in the right spot. *This girl is careful and exacting—she wants things in just the right order, but her family is anything but.* Maggie thought about the first summer after Richard's passing. All of a sudden, Emily had no father at one of the most crucial times in her life—her teen years when she was at a crossroads of trying to decide what to do and where to go. Maggie didn't have all the answers, and when she tried to talk with Emily, there had been many disagreements and many evenings of dead silence.

Then Maggie had an idea. "Magenta, do you work at the library full time? I mean, would you be interested in a part-time job? I see that you're quite particular about things, and I appreciate that quality in a person. I inherited a big house here in town, and I could use some help organizing some things that my aunt left behind."

Magenta stopped lining up books and turned around to look Maggie in the eyes. Her face held a hint of hope. "Yeah? Like, for money?"

"Probably minimum wage."

"That'd be really cool." Magenta looked thoughtful for a moment. "I'll have to ask Aunt Maura. She might even be relieved. When I got here last week, she said she didn't know what she was going to do with me all summer."

Maggie could see the hurt return to Magenta's eyes and tried to put herself in the girl's shoes. While Maggie knew she couldn't fix the past for Magenta, perhaps she could give her some positive memories to take back with her.

"We'll get it worked out, okay?"

"That'd be awesome. Thanks." Magenta gave Maggie a quick, shy smile. Something seemed to catch her eye, and she pointed to a desk nearby that was topped with an old-fashioned brass lamp with a green glass shade. "Oh, I think those are the books she pulled out for you." Without another word, she turned on her heel and walked off in the direction of the front counter.

Ah, youth. Maggie went to the desk Magenta had indicated, where a stack of about half a dozen books sat. She read each title, then grabbed the two books she thought would be most helpful to her. She carried her discards to a reshelving cart against the wall, then brought the winners to the checkout counter.

It appeared that Maura, Pearl, and Magenta were still in the thick of training, but Maura stepped away from the computer to help Maggie check out her books. "Will any of those work?"

"Yes, thanks, I hope these two will. Thanks so much for pulling them."

"Anytime," Maura said. "What did you decide to do with that dress?"

Maggie told Maura about displaying the gown in the antiques shop window and how every customer had seemed to want it thus far. "It's a piece of Aunt Evelyn's history that I'd like to figure out. There's a reason she kept it. I just sense that it's supposed to help me make an important connection to her past—to our family's past. And I can't help but think that much of the key to the story relates to that torn veil."

Maura was about to reply when the library phone rang at the counter. As Maura reached for the receiver, Maggie caught an abrupt movement out of the corner of her eye. When Maura had turned in her direction, Pearl had startled and knocked over a pencil cup on the desk. The woman's cheeks reddened as she gathered the pens and replaced them in the cup, and then she faced the computer. *Was she listening to our conversation?*

Maura seemed stuck on the phone with someone who wanted to donate books to the library and wouldn't take no for an answer. Maggie waited for a minute or so to see if she could talk to her about Magenta working part time for Maggie, but when she noticed the time, she decided it might be best to call Maura later instead.

Maggie looked around for Magenta so she could say goodbye, but the girl was nowhere to be seen. As she gathered her books from the counter, she said, "It was nice to meet you, Pearl."

The older woman's eyes never left the computer screen, but she gave an almost imperceptible nod.

As Maggie walked away, however, she felt Pearl watching her. It was most curious. Why would Pearl Winters be interested in Maggie's discussion with Maura about Aunt Evelyn and her dress?

Maggie decided to walk home via Shoreline Drive so that she could enjoy glimpses of the sunlight sparkling on the ocean. As she headed down toward the business district, she caught sight of James coming her way.

He smiled as he approached her. "I see I'm going in the right direction."

"James, I am so sorry I left you with those two ladies. How did things turn out?"

"First I got quite an earful about how Harriet acquires her clothing. Online, auctions, cross-country travels to other thrift stores. We were somewhere between Ohio and West Virginia when Maxine MacDonald marched over."

"I bet that was interesting," Maggie said.

"After a few initial hysterics, I was able to get the two women to sit down and discuss the matter of their near accident. When both women were finished talking, I summarized for them what I had heard them say."

"And?"

"Eventually, they pretty much agreed that they were both driving too quickly, and neither had anticipated someone coming from the other direction. Harriet agreed to drop the reckless driving charges against Maxine. Maxine even offered to wash Beulah or let her try a transporter for free."

"I see Harriet now has everyone on a first-name basis with her car," Maggie said. "You are a true diplomat, Mr. Alderman."

"Anything to keep peace in town," James said. "Sometimes it's just a matter of listening not only to what people say but also to what may be behind their words—their perceptions or motivations."

That remark struck a chord with Maggie, as she felt she had done just that with Magenta in the library. But rather than go into all that with James, she pointed to the briefcase in his hand and said, "In business mode, are we?"

"As a matter of fact, I'm headed to the municipal building for a permit."

"Far be it from me to slow down progress."

"You're never an unwelcome distraction," James said. "But I'll see you later."

They said goodbye and continued on their original paths. A block later, Maggie found herself in front of A Fine Vintage, where she noticed that the paper that had previously covered the front window had been removed. She stopped to admire the display of antique wedding dresses framed by gathered tulle curtains. Harriet had arranged the mannequins in what appeared to be chronological order. A turn-of-the-century-style dress with a high neck, long sleeves, and cinched waist was at far left. A 1940s-style satin gown with a sweetheart neckline and tapered sleeves was next, followed by a tea-length dress with a full skirt and a lace overlay, which Maggie thought probably dated to the 1960s. Dresses that looked like they were from the later part of the 1900s rounded out the variety. Maggie had to admit that her mystery dress would certainly fit nicely into the mix.

Completing the window display was a fainting sofa dotted with accessories such as gloves, jewelry, and clutch handbags. In the corner of the window hung a chalkboard sign that read *Opening in 3 Days* in cursive. The numeral was written atop a transparent white film of chalk, indicating that Harriet had been changing the number each day in a countdown.

Maggie peered around the dresses and tried to catch a glimpse of the rest of the shop. Harriet had a gift for decorating, that was for sure. Maggie saw Harriet farther back in the shop, hanging clothes and arranging things just so. Maggie straightened and considered leaving. *Do I really want another confrontation with her today?*

Harriet suddenly stopped and turned toward the window. Maggie held her hand up in a slight wave.

Harriet held up an index finger as if to say, "Just a minute." She took something into a back room, then came to the front door. She unlocked and opened the door but poked only her head out.

"Can I help you?" Her facial expression had softened from the hostility of earlier in the day to something that seemed more like nervousness to Maggie.

"No, not really. I was just admiring your window display. It was a lovely surprise to see it unveiled as I walked by."

"I had the windows covered with paper for the last month. It was a real mess in here, and I wanted everything to look just right before I let people see it."

"Is this your first shop, Harriet? It seems you know the business."

"Just following my instincts," Harriet said. "I grew up in a big family with eight adopted children, including myself. Our parents could never afford to buy clothing from a regular retail store, so we always shopped in thrift stores—you know, well before it was common or even popular like it is today. As a girl, I always looked a little faded, about ten years behind whatever was in style. But we had a lot of love that covered that all up and we toughed it out."

Maggie started to speak, but Harriet cut her off abruptly.

"Look, Maggie, unless you're here to tell me you changed your mind about the flapper dress, I can't spend all day shooting the breeze. I've got a lot to get done here."

"I'm afraid not," Maggie said. "The dress is just not for sale."

"If you say so." Harriet's head and shoulders disappeared, and she slammed and locked the door.

6

The next morning passed quickly in the shop, where Maggie and June saw a steady stream of customers. Many folks from town came by to see the new star of the Carriage House Antiques front window, having spotted the flyer for the wedding dress contest posted at The Busy Bean. Unfortunately, none of the lookie-loos seemed to have any new information.

When customer traffic quieted down in the early afternoon, Maggie decided to visit Ruth at the historical society to see what she could dig up about Somerset Harbor in the 1920s, and whether or not there had been a wedding planned for Sedgwick Manor at the time.

Sunlight shining through leafy maple trees cast mottled shadows on the rose-and-teal Victorian house that held the historical society museum. Walking up the sidewalk, Maggie watched the shadows on the white gingerbread trim change as the trees shimmied in the breeze.

Maggie found Ruth in the foyer of the painted lady, tidying a table full of pamphlets about local Civil War reenactments and historical farms in the area. "Good afternoon, Ruth," she said brightly.

Ruth glanced up and smiled. A few tendrils of hair stuck out at odd angles from her head. "Good afternoon to you."

"What happened to your shirt?" Maggie pointed to a tan streak smeared across Ruth's white button-down shirt.

"Good heavens, what now?" Ruth looked down, then at the table she was straightening. "Ugh, peanut butter on the table."

Maggie grimaced. "Do I dare ask?"

Ruth sighed, then grabbed a paper towel and cleaning solution from a nearby table and cleaned up the mess. "Our group of kids from yesterday seemed to have had a little trouble behaving since it's the last week of school. Most of them were good, but a few were much more interested in knocking over furniture and, apparently, smearing peanut butter on it for good measure."

"Can I help at all?"

"You're sweet to offer, but I've got it covered. I may need to run home and change my shirt, though." Ruth tossed the paper towel into the trash and patted her hair back into place. "What brings you by, Maggie?"

"I'm on a mission to find out more about my dress. I thought maybe I could look through the records room and see if there were any marriage licenses or wedding announcements or anything of the sort that relate to Sedgwick Manor in the 1920s."

"Sounds like fun," Ruth said. "I'll take you upstairs and get you started."

"I knew I came to the right place," Maggie said, then followed Ruth up the main staircase, each step creaking softly under her feet. Ruth led her through a door and up another flight of stairs to the attic, which was lined with shelf after shelf of cardboard boxes containing town records.

Maggie surveyed the room, daunted by the volume of carefully labeled cartons. "I always forget how overwhelming this place is."

"You just need to know where to look, my dear." Ruth walked over to a shelf along the side wall and pointed to a box labeled *Marriage Licenses 1922–1929.*

"There's a good reason you're in charge," Maggie said, joining Ruth. She removed the box from the shelf and carried it to a table in the center of the attic. "Speaking of which, I hope you're looking forward to your anniversary lunch on Thursday."

"I still think you girls are making a big fuss about nothing. I've been president of the historical society for fifteen years, not queen of England."

"You know us, Ruth. Any excuse to have a party." Maggie raised the lid off of the cardboard carton and assessed the organized but plentiful paperwork inside. "This could take awhile."

"Yes, but just think how exciting it will be when you find what you're looking for." Ruth pointed at the stain on her shirt. "While you're here, do you mind if I go home and change? You should be able to hear the doorbell from up here if anyone comes by to view the museum."

"I'd be happy to." Maggie pulled out a handful of papers from the box.

Ruth made to leave, then pulled at her shirt collar. "It's a little stuffy in here, isn't it? I'll open the windows before I go to let in some air." She opened windows on either side of the room to create a cross breeze, then approached the stairs. "I'll come see how you're doing when I get back."

"Thanks, Ruth," Maggie said with a wave, then turned her attention to the stack of marriage licenses in front of her. She checked each one to see if the bride's or groom's address matched Sedgwick Manor, or if she recognized their names from her family tree. She smiled when she came across familiar surnames as she leafed through the licenses—Linton, McGillis, Harper, Bennett—but she didn't find anyone named Sedgwick or McCrary, her mother's maiden name.

Maggie was about halfway through the box when she heard a very faint ringing. *The doorbell.* She set aside the papers she had in her hand and rushed down from the attic.

A little out of breath by the time she reached the foyer, Maggie took a moment to compose herself. She opened the door and was surprised to find Pearl Winters there with a small stack of books in her arms.

"Pearl, hi!" Maggie said cheerfully, then realized her enthusiasm did not quite match the woman's dour expression. Maggie cleared her throat. "Sorry if you were waiting long. I was up in the attic."

"The attic?" Pearl seemed to perk up, but then her stoicism returned. "I'm here to see Ruth Harper."

"Ruth stepped out for a minute, but she'll be back shortly. Can I help you?"

"No, I am here for Ruth. Maura has sent me with three books she requested."

"Do you want to give them to me?"

"You don't work here."

"No, but I am a member of the historical society." When Pearl didn't respond, Maggie stepped back and opened the door the rest of the way. "Would you like to come in and wait? You can look around the museum if you like. I'll text Ruth and let her know you're here."

Pearl nodded once, then entered the house. She immediately strode to a glass case that held the town's charter, handwritten on yellowed parchment.

"That document is nearly three hundred years old," Maggie said as she tapped out the message to Ruth and sent it.

"I see."

"Our museum is small, but we have a wonderful collection of town artifacts."

"Huh."

"Is there anything in particular you might like to learn more about? I know you're new to town, so I'd be happy to share some of the things I thought were most interesting when I moved here."

"No thanks."

"All right," Maggie said, getting the distinct impression that Pearl hoped she'd leave. "I'll just leave you to it, then. If you need anything, I'll be upstairs."

Slightly unsettled by her interaction with Pearl, Maggie returned to the attic. She groaned when she saw that the stack of papers she'd set down before going to answer the door had been blown off the table and scattered on the floor.

The old pine floorboards creaked under her as she scrambled to collect the marriage licenses. Shadows cast by the trees outside the windows danced across the walls as the wind picked up, and the cross breeze ruffled her hair. She tucked the errant locks behind her ears, then sat at the table to try to reorganize the jumbled paperwork.

A creaking sound came from the staircase. Was someone there, or was it just the old Victorian house settling in the gathering wind?

"Hello?" Maggie called. She listened but heard nothing more. Another gust of wind blew her hair from behind her ears, and she tucked it back again in frustration, wishing she had something to hold it in place.

Maggie nearly jumped out of her seat when the attic door slammed shut with a bang. Shaking her head, she got up and closed the two windows Ruth had opened. Hoping the attic door would provide enough ventilation, she descended the stairs to reopen it. She placed her hand on the door's antique knob and tried to turn it, but the knob barely moved in her hand. She rattled the knob until the door shook, but it didn't budge.

Maggie rapped on the door with her knuckles. "Hello?" She knocked again, more loudly this time. "Can anybody hear me? I think I'm locked in!" Surely Pearl was in earshot if she was downstairs in the museum. Why wasn't she coming up to help?

The attic's stuffiness was already returning, and Maggie felt a little queasy as the air thickened with heat. She went back up the steps and opened one of the windows. As she leaned close to get a breath of fresh air, she saw a figure walking down the sidewalk, away from the historical society building. Pearl. Or the back of her, at least.

"Pearl!" Maggie called out, thinking perhaps she could come back and let her out of the attic.

But Pearl didn't react to Maggie's shouts.

Maggie patted her pockets for her cell phone so she could call Ruth, but her phone wasn't in her pockets or her purse. She had left it downstairs when she'd texted Ruth about Pearl's arrival.

Maggie returned to the bottom of the attic stairs and pounded on the door again. Beads of sweat started to form at her temples. She was trapped. It wasn't her first time, but somehow it was always terrifying.

She checked her watch. Ruth had been gone for at least half an hour already. What was taking her so long?

Maggie heard footsteps creaking down the second-floor hallway toward the attic door.

"Maggie?" Ruth called to her from the other side of the door, her voice muffled.

"Ruth! I can't get out."

"What?" The doorknob rattled. "The key is gone. Hold on, I'll be right back."

A few minutes later, the footsteps returned. Maggie heard the sound of metal on metal, then a click. The knob rattled again, but the door didn't move. After several more clicks, she called, "What's going on?"

"I thought the door was locked, but it still won't open," Ruth replied through the door. "And now I've lost track of whether I locked it or unlocked it. Can you push on it while I pull?"

"Sure, just tell me when."

"On three. One, two, three!"

Maggie pushed on the door, then used her shoulder to nudge it a little harder. At last the door gave way, and Maggie stumbled out into the second-floor hallway, with Ruth stepping back just in time to avoid a collision.

"Thank goodness, Ruth." Maggie breathed a sigh of relief. "The wind blew the door shut on me and I couldn't get it open. I was worried I was locked up here."

Ruth shook her head. "Must have been a combination of the humidity and these darn old doorknobs. But that doesn't explain . . ."

"What is it?"

"The key is missing. Somebody took it."

"Are you sure?" Maggie shivered despite the warm air. Not wanting to dwell, however, she didn't wait for Ruth's answer. "Regardless, thank you for rescuing me. I thought someone would have heard me yelling, but Pearl apparently didn't hear me shouting up here."

"Pearl?"

"Pearl Winters, Maura's new library volunteer. She came by to bring you some books you requested. I let her into the museum to wait for you." Maggie wiped her brow with the back of her hand. "You didn't see her?"

"No, nobody was here when I got back," Ruth said. "She must have gotten tired of waiting."

"Must have."

"So how did the researching go?" Ruth glanced up the stairs toward the attic. "Find anything useful?"

"Nothing at all," Maggie said. "And frankly, I think I'm a bit done for the day after this excitement."

"I don't blame you."

Maggie slumped when she remembered how the marriage licenses were now in total disarray. "The wind blew the files around something dreadful when I went to let Pearl in. I was in the middle of reorganizing them when the door shut."

Ruth waved a hand. "Don't worry a bit. I'll take care of it."

"Are you sure?"

"Of course. I have fifteen years of experience, remember?"

They chuckled, then Ruth propped the attic door open with a wooden stopper. Maggie followed her downstairs to the first floor. As she entered the foyer, she casually glanced at the framed black-and-white photographs and newspaper clippings hung on the wall. She stopped short when one in particular caught her eye. *Famed Designer Summers in Somerset Harbor* read the headline. Beneath the headline was a photograph of two men shaking hands. They stood in a white gazebo draped with patriotic bunting and wore what appeared to be seersucker suits.

Maggie read the caption out loud. "'Franklin Sedgwick welcomes renowned fashion designer Jean Patierre to Sedgwick Manor, July 4, 1928.' Ruth, this is the man who designed the wedding dress. And the man shaking his hand is my great-grandfather."

In addition to the wind picking up, the sky had darkened. Maggie quickened her pace as she walked home from the historical society building, hoping to beat the brewing storm. She thought about the article hung on the wall and how she now had definitive proof that someone in her family was tied to the dress, or at least its designer.

Ruth hadn't had much more information to share beyond what the article said. The Sedgwicks of the 1920s had been known for their extravagant Fourth of July parties, when they'd invite everyone from friends and family to local celebrities to hobnob at their home. Apparently, in 1928, the guest list had included famous French fashion designer Jean Patierre.

Maggie's thoughts were interrupted as she approached the front door of Sedgwick Manor and spotted a familiar face.

"Magenta, hi," Maggie said. "What a nice surprise. I was going to call your aunt as soon as I got in."

"Yeah, hi. Um, I asked Aunt Maura about working for you, and she's totally cool with it. Can I help you with anything right now?"

"I just got home, so I need a minute to think. Come on in, though." Maggie unlocked the front door and held it open for the girl. She watched Magenta's eyes widen when she caught sight of the impressive chandelier glittering overhead.

"Wow, this is some house."

"Thank you," Maggie said. "Let me give you a little tour, of the first floor at least."

Magenta followed Maggie silently through the kitchen,

breakfast room, living room, and master suite, seemingly taking it all in as Maggie told her a few interesting facts about the home.

"You must be, like, rich," Magenta said finally as they walked through the dining room.

Maggie smiled. She was used to people having that impression when they visited the manor. "It's a family estate that most recently belonged to my aunt, actually. Now I do my best to take good care of it."

"Must be a big job."

"It is, but my aunt made sure it would be doable before she passed. Speaking of jobs, I think it makes sense for you to start work in your comfort zone. Come on into the library, the last stop on the tour."

They made the short trek across the foyer to the library, where Magenta gave a soft gasp of wonder. She immediately went toward the closest bookshelf and started reading over the spines.

"You could go through the books in here and make a little better sense of them," Maggie said. "It may have been organized at some point, but I think it got a bit jumbled over the years. You could at least separate nonfiction from fiction."

"No problem," Magenta said. She picked up a framed photo of Maggie, Emily, and Richard resting on one of the shelves. "Is this your family?"

"Yes, that's my daughter, Emily. She's a nurse now, in Boston. That's my husband, Richard. He died several years ago."

"Bummer," Magenta said. "Sorry, I mean, that's too bad. How did you meet him?"

Maggie was slightly surprised that Magenta had asked that rather than how Richard had died, but she was happy to share. "We met in college. I was moving into a dorm room, and he offered to help carry my boxes for me. And the rest is history, as they say."

Magenta grinned. "I guess that's kinda romantic."

"In our way, I suppose so. You like romances, right? Like *Wuthering Heights*?"

Magenta shrugged. "I'm more into the intrigue side of that book—the darker, the better."

"Do any of the Brontës' novels have happy endings?"

Magenta thought for a moment. "Jane Eyre lives happily ever after. Sort of." She frowned. "It's complicated. You'll just have to read it for yourself. You know, I might find it in here. I'd be really surprised not to with this collection."

Just then lightning streaked across the sky toward the harbor, and about two seconds later thunder boomed overhead. Rain immediately started pouring on the house. They were in for a good soaking.

Magenta jumped and said, "I-I have to go. I told Aunt Maura I wouldn't be gone long." She started heading toward the foyer.

"But I thought you—" The slam of the front door cut off Maggie's words. Magenta was gone.

Shaking her head, Maggie looked at her watch and was surprised to see it was close to seven. After a busy couple of days, a quiet evening at home was in order. She reheated some chicken Alfredo and shared bits of the chicken with Snickers as she ate. Then she retired to her bed with her computer in her lap and the fashion history books spread in front of her.

The thunder had subsided, but the rain and wind continued. As raindrops pelted the windows, Maggie searched online for dresses that resembled her vintage wedding gown. One auction site showed authentic Roaring Twenties dresses less spectacular than Maggie's commanding bids of thousands of dollars.

Wow. Now that she had a ballpark of how valuable the dress could be, she was even more confused and conflicted. She closed her computer, set it aside, and began thumbing through the fashion books. Soon, however, her eyelids drooped and she dozed off.

• • • • • • • • • • • • • • • • •

Church bells rang loudly. Maggie stood at an altar in a swirling cloud of flower petals. She looked down and was surprised to see that she was wearing the flapper wedding dress. The halves of the torn veil floated in her peripheral vision on both sides. Ina, Ruth, June, and Liz gathered behind her wearing powder-blue bridesmaid's dresses. Maggie heard a door slam and turned toward the church's entrance. Down the aisle came a Segway with not Maxine but Harriet at the helm, wearing an Edgar Allan Poe T-shirt. Maggie felt a hand on her arm and turned to see Magenta next to her. Magenta opened her mouth to speak, but the only sound that came out was a meow . . .

Maggie awoke to find Snickers pacing in tight circles on her bed and mewing insistently. She glanced at the clock. *Almost nine already? How did I sleep so long?* She stacked her library books and laptop on the nightstand, then climbed out of bed.

As she took a quick shower and got dressed, Snickers continued to express impatience and displeasure. "I know, I know, it's breakfast time."

He followed her to the kitchen, where she filled his food dish, which seemed to mollify him slightly. Maggie glanced at her coffee maker, then decided it was a good morning to let someone else brew her coffee for her.

Fifteen minutes later, Maggie exited The Busy Bean holding two cups of Jamaican blend in a cardboard carrier and a small paper bag full of pastries. She figured she'd surprise June with breakfast since she'd probably been at the shop for a while now. The sidewalk was still a little wet from the previous night's rain, so she stepped carefully to avoid puddles.

Halfway home, Maggie caught sight of Maxine barreling

down the road toward her on her transporter. *She'd better be careful on these slick streets.* Helmeted head bent to one side, the woman was awkwardly balancing a large black plastic bag over her shoulder as she drove, though she kept up an impressively brisk speed despite her bulky load. She turned sharply onto a side street.

When Maggie crossed the intersection, she glanced in the direction Maxine had gone but saw no trace of her. It was as though she and her cargo had simply vanished.

Turning down the driveway to the antiques shop, Maggie suddenly felt a chill go up her spine. She shivered, and the cups in the cardboard drink carrier vibrated. The cold feeling grew the closer she got to the shop. When the carriage house came into view, she saw that her sense of dread wasn't unfounded.

The front door of the antiques shop stood wide open. The wind blew rainwater from nearby trees into the shop. But Maggie was focused on a much bigger problem.

The wedding dress was gone.

8

Maggie jogged the rest of the way down the lane and hurried into the store. "June?" she called out. Maybe June had accidentally left the door open. Maggie set the coffee and pastry bag on the counter, then went to the front window, heart pounding and mouth agape.

Just then June appeared at the door. "Hey, you're here early. You won't believe what just happened." June wiped her wet shoes on the entry mat and joined Maggie.

"Look." Maggie pointed to the window display, where an empty mannequin stood in a pile of cast-off accessories.

June gasped. "The dress, Maggie. Where is it?"

"The front door was open when I got here."

"I just ran to the bank." June's words were rushed as she explained her absence. "I finalized a huge sale right when I opened today. A woman bought that lovely Victorian bedroom set *and* the Queen Anne dining table and chairs. She paid in cash—more than $5,000 with tax—and I thought I'd better take it to the bank rather than leave a lot of large bills here on hand in the shop."

"That was smart, but . . ." Maggie found herself at a loss for words.

June examined the front door. "It wasn't forced open. But I locked it when I left. How did someone get in?"

Maggie and June decided to look through the shop to see if anything else had been taken. Maggie watched as June opened the register and counted all of the daily start-up cash. Everything was there.

June examined the glass display cases where some of the more valuable smaller items were kept.

Maggie wandered through the store. Nothing seemed to be missing. She walked to the oversize doors they used when moving large furniture in and out, but they were locked tight. She returned to the front counter, where June was wringing her hands.

"I don't see anything missing from the display cabinets. Or anywhere else, for that matter," June said. "Just the dress."

Maggie grimaced. "Maxine MacDonald and Harriet Hamstead were both very insistent about wanting it for themselves. I hate to call them suspects, but they both acted very peculiar the other day."

June agreed. "And then there was Pearl Winters."

"Pearl?" Maggie asked. "As in Pearl the new library volunteer? When did you meet her?"

"She's the one who bought all the furniture this morning. She's been coming in for weeks, looking at it and then leaving, but she finally sealed the deal. She wasn't here long—just long enough to pay for the items with a huge wad of cash. And long enough to notice the wedding dress and ask if she could try it on."

"Try it on?" Maggie asked. "Is she getting married?"

"No, she just muttered something about buying the dress and the mannequin for a display piece in her home. I don't know if I'd use it as decor personally, but to each her own."

"But why would Pearl ask to try the dress on if she just wanted to display it?"

"No idea."

"Okay. Let's think. How long were you gone?"

"There was just one teller open at the bank, and the elementary school principal brought in a bucketful of change from the last Pennies for Patients drive right before I got there."

"Don't tell me they were counting pennies right there at the bank window?" Maggie said.

"No, she was just getting the paper sleeves for them. But when she went to grab the bucket from the counter, the handle gave way and the coins fell all over the floor. We crawled around for a good ten minutes picking them up." June looked at Maggie, her eyes glistening. "I'm so sorry. I thought I'd just be five minutes. It turned out to be more than twenty, I think."

Maggie sighed. "It's not your fault, June. But I think it's time I call the police."

A few minutes later, after relating the basic facts of the case to the dispatcher, Maggie hung up the phone. "Robert Linton will be over as soon as he can."

June nodded. "Speaking of Lintons, Ina was in here yesterday taking photos of the dress and asking me about trying it on too. Well, her and about three other women of a certain age."

"Why does everyone want to try it on?" Maggie huffed in exasperation. She picked up her cup from the cardboard carrier and took a drink. It was lukewarm, but at least it was coffee.

June took a drink from the other cup, then set it back down. "I don't know about Ina, but in the other ladies' case, I think it's to do with that Dancing With the Seniors competition at the VFW."

"Competition?"

"My mom and dad are really into it," June said. "The senior group that meets there has a dance instructor who comes in every week, and everyone had so much fun with the classes that they decided to basically have a Charleston dance-off Friday night."

Maggie laughed as she put down her coffee cup. "I bet that'll be a riot."

"I know," June said. "Mom said that Dad has two left feet, but at least it gets them out of the house doing something every week that gets their heart rates up. She said that lots of couples are going to do it, and people are even making costumes."

"Sounds like a ton of fun," Maggie said.

"Why don't you come with me to watch? Mom and Dad would love to have you there for moral support."

"Sure, why not? I don't have any plans, and maybe I can learn a few steps."

Just then the front door opened, and in walked Officer Linton. He removed his cap to reveal his boyish, freckled face. "Hello, ladies."

"Good morning, Robert," June said. "Sorry to drag you out on a soggy day like this."

"Not as sorry as I am to hear you've had a burglary," Robert said. "Why don't you tell me what happened from the beginning."

Maggie and June filled him in on the details. When Maggie had finished describing how she had found the door open and the dress missing that morning, they all went to the front display window. Robert asked questions about what had been disturbed and continued jotting down notes.

"Got any ideas about who would have a motive for taking the dress?" Robert asked. "It seems a bit peculiar to me because, as you mentioned, the cash was left in the register, and anyone could have opened that thing."

Maggie and June told him about everyone who had asked to try on the dress or buy it, including Harriet, Maxine, Pearl, and, to Robert's amusement, his aunt Ina.

June gazed into space for a moment. "There was something peculiar that Pearl Winters mentioned this morning. After she asked about the dress, I said it could be the focal point for a beautiful wedding—a perfect one. And then she said, 'Weddings are never picture-perfect. There's always something that goes wrong.' She stared at the dress when she said that, as though she were remembering something. It was an odd moment. I didn't know what to say."

Maggie chose not to mention that she didn't think there was a way to say the right thing to the rather impassive Pearl Winters.

"It is odd, but speculation about what someone might be thinking isn't evidence," Robert said. "Can you get me the sales records from the last couple of days? I want to look at that after I dust for fingerprints."

While June was making copies of the week's receipts, Robert went to his squad car to retrieve his fingerprinting equipment and supplies, then came back to the shop. After he had dusted for prints on any nearby hard surfaces, he put the equipment back in his car and returned to the front counter with clipboard and pen in hand.

"Any idea of what the dress is worth?" he asked Maggie.

"I've done some research on it," she said. "I didn't find anything exactly like it online, but dresses of similar quality from that era seemed to be selling for anywhere between $4,000 and $10,000. Even more importantly, it was my aunt's, so I wouldn't be able to put a price tag on its sentimental value."

"It was an expensive loss then," Officer Linton said.

Maggie nodded. "It was made by a well-known designer and could be one of a kind."

"It'll be challenging to file an insurance claim," June said, handing the receipt copies to Robert.

He tucked the photocopies inside his clipboard. "Do either of you have a photograph of the dress?"

Maggie said she did, but when she checked her phone, the battery was dead.

"I took a few photos this morning," June said, "right after Pearl left and before I went to the bank. My daughters love *The Great Gatsby*, so I wanted to show them the dress."

June pulled her phone out of her pocket and brought up the photo gallery. She handed the device to Robert. He scrolled through the pictures, then stopped at the last one. After staring for a moment, he enlarged it with his fingers.

"June, where did you take this photo?" he asked quietly.

June pointed to an oak wardrobe with a full-length side mirror resting nearby. "I was getting a glare from the window glass, so I moved the mannequin over by that wardrobe for better lighting. Why?"

"Take a look at the mirror in the photo," he said.

June and Maggie examined the photograph, then gasped in unison.

The mirror showed a pair of eyes peering from behind a tapestry across the room.

9

Maggie looked from the image on the phone's screen to the corner of the shop where the tapestry hung. The intricately woven textile featured a pastoral setting of trees overlooking an expansive soft blue river. A single figure—a young woman with long brown hair and a flowing, ankle-length white gown with gold trim—stood facing the river as though waiting for someone. Hers were the only eyes Maggie saw now, but she remained chilled by the photograph.

"Any chance you recognize that pair of eyes?" Officer Linton asked.

"No," June said. "They're not very clear. Do you, Maggie?"

Maggie shook her head. "No, sorry."

"I took those photos right before leaving, so that means there was probably someone in the store when I left. Which is why the door was open but not forced open, even though I'd locked up." June bit her lip. "I was so busy working on the big sale to Pearl, someone could have come into the shop without me knowing. I didn't even think about checking for other customers before I left. I just snapped those last couple of photos and took off for the bank."

Officer Linton said he could enlarge the images even more at the police station and asked June to send the photos to him via e-mail.

Maggie had a thought. "What if I offer a reward for the return of the dress? We were running a contest for whoever could tell us its history. I could offer a reward now instead. Maybe a hundred dollars? Would anyone respond, do you think?"

"Rewards often don't provide enough incentive for anyone to return lost or stolen items. If there's a reward out for it, they know it's valuable, so they'll usually try to see what a pawnshop or something will give for it. Is that what it's worth to you, Maggie? One hundred dollars?"

Maggie knew it was certainly worth more than that to her. "I'm convinced that the dress has family significance. In that respect, I suppose it's technically priceless."

"I'd suggest holding off on a reward until I've made some headway on the investigation," Officer Linton said. "For now, you can go back to business as usual."

Maggie sighed. "Whatever that means. Are you okay here, June? I'd like to run back to the house for a bit."

"Of course, take your time," June said. "I'll just see what I can do about fixing up our window display. I think we have an antique dressing gown we can put on the mannequin for the time being."

"Thanks, June. You're a trooper." Maggie turned to Officer Linton. "I'll walk you out, Robert."

After saying goodbye to Officer Linton, who promised to be in touch if he heard anything, Maggie headed home through the small woods between Carriage House Antiques and Sedgwick Manor. As she walked along, she realized she hadn't told Officer Linton about the torn veil, though she wasn't sure if it would have any bearing on his investigation. She also remembered seeing Maxine zipping down the street with a large black garbage bag right before arriving at the shop to find it burglarized. *Robert's got plenty to do. Maybe I could talk to Maxine myself.*

A few minutes later, Maggie entered the side door of the manor and collapsed on the living room sofa. Snickers hopped up into her lap, and she tried to relax as she scratched behind his ears to his apparent delight. However, names and faces kept swirling through her head, and she recalled the unsettling dream she'd awakened from earlier that morning.

The doorbell sounded, breaking into Maggie's thoughts. She pushed herself up off the sofa and walked to the front door, which she opened to find a smiling James wearing gray running shorts and a plain navy T-shirt. In his hands was a small bouquet of white daisies in green tissue paper.

"You heard," she said.

"Yes," he said. "Ina got the report on her police scanner. She saw me out running, so she stopped me and filled me in. It just so happens that The Singing Mermaid was on my route, and I thought you could use a pick-me-up."

"I'm touched. Thank you," Maggie said, taking the flowers from his outstretched hand.

"So, Carriage House Antiques was burglarized?"

"My wedding dress was stolen. I mean, the flapper dress."

"So now it's doubly mysterious," James said. "Where it came from and where it has gone. Are you okay? I wondered if you felt safe, if you wanted anyone close by."

"It's kind of you to worry, but I'm not concerned about anyone breaking into the house, if that's what you mean."

"That's good," James said. "And your visitor just now didn't add to your jumble of problems?"

"What visitor?" Maggie said. "No one's been here since I got home."

"When I was walking up to the house, I saw someone running through the woods from the house toward the shop. I thought it might have been you at first, but then I realized it wasn't."

"Did you get a good look?"

"Afraid not. It was just a dark blur amongst the trees by the time I focused on it."

"What if that person had something to do with the burglary?" Maggie asked. "Let's go to the shop. We should tell June, at least."

Maggie set the flowers on the porch, and the two of them headed toward the carriage house. It was only midday, but gray clouds still hung over the harbor and town, and it almost felt as if dusk had fallen early. Rain was not threatening anymore, but a coolness had set in and fog was rising up from the ocean, turning the trees and buildings of the landscape into fuzzy and ethereal shapes.

As they walked through the thin woods, Maggie elaborated about the discovery of the missing dress and Robert Linton's investigation. She hugged herself and rubbed her upper arms as they approached the building. "I know this isn't the first time something has been stolen from the shop, but it just seems to hit home a little more. That dress is special."

"Then we'll do our best to track it down," James said. "You check the front, Maggie. I'll look around the outside of the shop."

The bell tinkled as Maggie walked through the front door. June was just putting the finishing touches on the redone window display. "Any news?"

Maggie walked toward her. "Not really. James just stopped by and said he saw someone running this way from Sedgwick Manor." Maggie looked around. No one else was there.

"We haven't had any customers since you left," June said. "Maybe the gray weather is keeping them away."

The front door opened and James stepped in. "Everything is fine around the building," he said. "The cargo doors are secure, and I didn't see anything or anyone suspicious."

"June, I think I'll take the rest of the day to see if I can find out any more about the history of the dress. Maybe that will help us figure out who stole it. Let me know if anything comes up, okay?"

"Of course. I'll hold down the fort. Good luck."

After one last look around the shop, Maggie and James headed back to the manor. At the front door, James picked up the flowers and handed them to her again. "So, what's the first step in researching the dress?"

"I thought I would look through the family albums to see if there is a photo of anyone wearing the dress."

"Didn't you say it had never been worn?"

"I don't think it has. It's in perfect condition, but maybe whoever wore it was just really careful not to spill." Maggie smiled and shrugged. "It's a start anyway."

"Tell me if I can help. You know where to find me."

"Sure do." Maggie thanked James for the flowers again and said goodbye. She headed to the kitchen for a vase. She grabbed a cobalt-blue pitcher, arranged the daisies in it one by one, and filled the pitcher with water. Then she set the pitcher in the center of the sunny yellow cloth on the breakfast room table and smiled. Daisies always brought summer into the house and into her heart.

After a quick lunch, Maggie felt reenergized, so she headed to the library to go through Evelyn's family photo albums. She went to the bookshelf that held the albums, thinking briefly about how nice it would be once Magenta had organized the bookshelves. *If she ever comes back.* Brushing away the memory of the girl's abrupt departure the night before, Maggie pulled out a stack of photo albums and sat down with them in the Regency chair near the fireplace.

The top album in the stack had the most recent photos in it, including many of Maggie as a young girl visiting Sedgwick Manor for the summer. Here were Uncle George and Aunt Evelyn on vacation at the Grand Canyon. There was a family reunion in the late 1980s.

She set that album aside and pulled out the next one, in which the McCrary sisters—Aunt Evelyn; Maggie's mom, Annette; and their younger sister, Sharon—were pictured as brides and young mothers. The next album showed the girls as poodle-skirted teenagers in the late '50s, and the album after that as young girls in pinafores.

Maggie thought briefly about calling Aunt Sharon to see if she knew anything about the history of the dress. However, Sharon was a modernist who did not share her sister's love of the past or antiques. *If Evelyn didn't leave any clues about the history of the dress, I can't imagine Sharon would know much.*

Maggie kept turning the pages through that album, then went on to the next, which was from her grandmother's generation. Here were faces and places not as familiar to Maggie. She came across her grandparents' wedding photo. Her grandmother wore a shiny silk gown with long sleeves that ballooned at the top and tapered into fitted points on the backs of her hands. *I don't understand why such pretty sleeves have such an unattractive name as "leg of mutton."* The dress had a long train, at least five feet, and the voluminous veil extended just as far. *A little different from a calf-length flapper dress with a fringed hem,* Maggie thought with amusement. In addition to a photo of just her grandparents on their wedding day, there was an image of the bride and groom with presumably their families. There beside her grandmother was Franklin Sedgwick, looking dapper in a single-button suit, long tie, and high-waisted trousers.

Maggie kept paging through the album. Many of the photos featured what seemed to be summer vacations at the shore from her grandmother's childhood in Maine, perhaps at Ogunquit Beach. The landmarks were somewhat familiar. Ladies in ruffled bathing clothes that fully covered them dipped their toes in the chilly Atlantic. Men waded in to knee-deep in the lapping waves. Children built castles in the sand. Life seemed simpler then. But Maggie knew that much of the 1920s was spent trying to forget the horrible effects of World War I. She imagined there were all kinds of sorrowful stories behind the smiles.

She turned the pages, studying each image, until she reached the end of the album, where a final photo was tucked into the back. It was loose and sideways, not lined up and adhered in place like the rest of the photos. She peered closely at the image. The photo looked like the one in the newspaper clipping that Maxine had showed her the other day—only it appeared to be the original. In it, a young woman was wearing the flapper wedding dress, including the veil. But on her face was no bridal glow. Instead, the woman looked absolutely grief-stricken.

· · · · · · · · · · · · · · · · ·

Maggie couldn't figure out how to drive the Segway. She had found the wedding dress in a black plastic bag at The Busy Bean. Now she had to get the dress back to the antiques shop, but she was having the hardest time holding the dress and driving the vehicle. When she wanted to go forward, it went backward. When she wanted to turn left, it went right. And everywhere she looked, someone was trying to run her down or get in her path. Maxine MacDonald was chasing her on her own scooter. Harriet Hamstead was beeping at her from behind the wheel of her Bel Air. And little Ina kept trying to jump on and ride with her.

Maggie only wanted to get to the antiques shop to make sure everything was okay. As she tried to figure out how to steer the vehicle, the dress flew out of the bag and wrapped itself around her head. As she frantically fought to free herself from the dress, she saw that the patroller was heading for a cliff. She saw James at the last second, yelling, "Stop, Maggie!"

But it was too late. The transporter flew off the cliff with her on it.

Maggie awoke in a sweat. But there was no dress draped across her face. Instead, it was Snickers's tail. He was trying to get comfortable on her pillow next to her head. And she wasn't flying off a cliff—she was hanging off the edge of the bed.

Maggie pulled herself back up fully onto the mattress and under the handmade quilt in soft pastels that she had just brought out for summer. Snickers relocated himself from the pillow to her lap.

Maggie's strange dream had rattled her, but a glance out the window lifted her spirits. It was a beautiful day. The fog had lifted, and the sun had burned off the last dreary vestiges. Birds were chatting away cheerily as they hunted for breakfast on the ground just outside her window.

After Maggie got ready for the day, she fixed a small breakfast and then sat down with her eggs, toast, and coffee at the breakfast table. While she ate, she made a mental to-do list. In addition to checking in with June and Officer Linton, she wanted to go to the opening of A Fine Vintage. There was still something odd about the fact that Harriet was featuring wedding dresses in her window display—and Maggie's heirloom had been stolen just yesterday.

As she took a sip of coffee, Maggie's thoughts landed on the black plastic bag in her nightmare. Certainly that part of her dream had been inspired by yesterday's near encounter with Maxine as she'd driven around town carrying an overstuffed garbage bag. Could Maxine have been in the shop when June left for the bank yesterday? Were those her eyes haunting June's photo of the wedding dress? And had she taken the gown? A car in the parking lot would have told June there was a customer in the shop, but it would have been fairly easy for Maxine to hide her transporter around the side of the carriage house so June wouldn't notice it.

Maggie finished her coffee and stood to clear her plate. *I don't want to go making accusations prematurely, but it's definitely worth a chat with Maxine.*

Maggie figured she could stop by A Fine Vintage and then go to Maxine's before Ruth's anniversary lunch at The Busy Bean. Although they'd certainly honor Ruth, Maggie knew that they'd likely spend a good amount of time discussing the missing wedding dress. Word had very likely spread to all members of the historical society by now, and her friends were always good for a brainstorming session when there was a mystery involved.

Last but not least, Maggie knew she needed to give Emily a call sometime during the day to see how her apartment lease signing had gone. *She'll be up in arms when I tell her about the dress.*

After cleaning up, Maggie grabbed her purse and walked to Carriage House Antiques. She found that June had completely redone the front window and was dressing the mannequin in a series of vintage aprons, one layered over the top of another. Maggie smiled. She was always drawn to vintage aprons with their cheery floral or gingham prints. They reminded her of Aunt Evelyn, who had kept many on hand for tasks around the kitchen.

"Good morning, June."

June waved half-heartedly. The shop manager looked smart in her white capris and a blue-and-white striped top, but she seemed a little down.

"I love what you're doing here with the display," Maggie said, though she was a little unsure why June had decided to start from scratch. "It's very summery."

June sighed. "Thanks. I know it's silly to change out the whole thing, but the dressing gown I tried on the mannequin yesterday just didn't fit in. It wasn't the same without the wedding dress. I still feel awful."

"It's really not your fault."

"I couldn't stop thinking about it all night long. I searched community sale websites in the area in case someone's trying to sell it online—all the way down to Providence, Rhode Island, and all the way over to Albany, New York. I didn't find anything. I'll keep checking over the next few days, though."

"I might have something that will cheer you up."

June looked at her expectantly.

Maggie smiled. "I found a photo in one of Evelyn's albums of a woman wearing the dress."

"You didn't!"

"I did. And the oddest thing is that Maxine MacDonald showed me a photo from a newspaper the other day that looked very similar. Unfortunately, all that's written on the back of mine is *Photographed by Ralph Finn*, so I still have no idea who was wearing it."

"That's still something. At least you're on the right track." June finished tying a bow on the last apron and stood back to gaze critically at her work.

"I figure I'll stop by Maxine's house later and ask her to show me her photograph again," Maggie said. "She was rather brusque the other day, but maybe she'll tell me the story behind her picture. Before that, though, I want to stop by the opening day reception at A Fine Vintage. At least when I see Harriet this time, I can tell her there's no way for me to sell her the dress since it has been stolen."

"You don't think she's the one who stole it, do you?" June adjusted some 1940s jadeite bowls she'd set up on a table near the apron-bedecked mannequin.

"I don't know what to think, but I do know that you'll be the first to know if I figure out who our burglar is."

After the women said goodbye, Maggie walked up the shop's driveway. As she did, an out-of-state car was coming the other way, toward the antiques shop. Glad to see customers en route to the shop, Maggie waved a friendly hello.

A few minutes later, she approached the small crowd gathered in front of A Fine Vintage. *I guess a lot of people had the same idea.* She joined the others there, including several ladies she recognized from Old Faith Chapel.

After a few pleasantries, one of the ladies said, "I heard a vintage wedding dress was stolen from your shop. Simply awful. Will you be able to collect on your insurance, Maggie?"

"A Roaring Twenties dress, I heard," another church friend said. "That must have been quite the unusual find. Where did you get it?"

Maggie just smiled and nodded, trying not to give away too many details. *Not that I have that many details to give.*

At precisely ten o'clock, Harriet unlocked the front door and rolled out a clothing rack topped with a sign that read *Irresistibles.* On the rack were about a dozen summer dresses in an array of jewel tones. "Excuse me, please," she said as she wheeled the rack into place in front of the shop. "Welcome, everyone."

Harriet returned to the shop door and held it open for her customers. As the crowd of about twenty customers, mostly women, filed in, Maggie had to admit that Harriet looked fantastic. Her black cotton button-up blouse had a high, tapered collar and long sleeves folded up once and pressed crisply in place. *Very 1950s Parisian,* Maggie mused. In any case, it went perfectly with the full black-and-white striped skirt that fell just below her knees. Maggie loved that Harriet went light on her jewelry—her pixie haircut showed off just a pair of red clip-on earrings that echoed the red of her high heels. She greeted each customer warmly at the door.

One of the church ladies complimented her on her outfit.

"Thank you," Harriet said so all could hear. "If you like what I've got on, you've come to the right place."

Despite her initial impressions of Harriet the other day, Maggie could hardly wait to get into the store. And when she finally got inside—slipping through behind another customer who had captured Harriet's attention—she certainly was not disappointed. A vintage rattan cart stood just inside the door with an insulated coffee dispenser and charmingly mismatched china teacups, as well as a tray of miniature scones she suspected were from The Busy Bean. Still full from breakfast, she resisted the temptation to take a scone, but she thought the refreshments were a lovely touch.

As Maggie looked around, she saw ladies going through long racks of dresses, blouses, and skirts. A few customers studied the backs of the wedding dresses displayed in the window, as though appreciating a museum exhibit.

One woman said, "I remember my sister wearing a dress like this when she got married in the '60s."

Another said, "What about these poufy sleeves of the 1980s and '90s? Weren't they something?"

Maggie remembered the dress she'd worn to marry Richard in the same time period. That lady was right—*poufy* had been popular: poufy sleeves, poufy shoulders, poufy skirts, and even poufy hair. She smiled as a nostalgic feeling washed over her.

Maggie started browsing along one long rack of everyday dresses and evening gowns and discovered several promising items to try on. She picked up a lovely sheath in a summery salmon shade and draped the dress over her arm. On top of that, she added a matching cardigan-and-shell set in a soft yellow and a white skirt with a lace overlay.

"That skirt would be just right to wear on a date with your favorite bachelor." Ina had appeared at Maggie's elbow and was inspecting the clothing in her hands.

"Hi there. On the job today?" Maggie asked, noticing the now-ever-present notepad and pen in Ina's hand.

"Among other things," Ina said. "This is quite the grand opening, wouldn't you say?"

"It sure is. Harriet certainly has a flair for style and a knack for presentation. She has so much lovely clothing, it'll be hard to walk away with just a few pieces." As she watched Ina jot down notes, she realized that her remarks would likely end up on the record.

"Nothing quite as nice as your wedding dress though. Any news on your burglary yesterday?"

Maggie straightened. As much as she loved Ina, she didn't feel comfortable sharing any details with the readership of *The Somerset Harbor Herald.* "Nothing new to report, Ina. You might want to ask your nephew about the investigation."

"Yeah, I tried that. He told me he didn't think it was appropriate to share the details of an ongoing criminal investigation, even with his favorite aunt." Ina sounded slightly put out, though Maggie was hardly surprised that Officer Linton had been less than forthcoming. He was a professional, after all. She admired his backbone, considering how persuasive Ina could be.

"I suppose I'd best be on my way," Ina said, putting her notepad away in her fanny pack. "Though I did see some lovely silver sandals up near the front I might try on."

Maggie looked down at Ina's sturdy walking shoes, which she was wearing with khaki shorts that reached her knees and a plaid camp shirt with sleeves rolled up to her elbows. She couldn't remember ever seeing Ina in anything but practical clothing. "Special occasion coming up?"

Ina waved her hand dismissively. "No time to chat, Maggie. See you later." And with that, Ina disappeared into the crowd.

Feeling the weight of the clothes in her arms, Maggie looked around for a dressing room. She saw two areas at the back of the shop covered in black-and-white polka-dot curtains, but both had a line three or four women deep. As Maggie scanned the store, she saw another set of the same curtains.

Dodging other shoppers, she walked over and pulled the curtains aside, then took one step through. Maggie instantly realized that the area was not a dressing room at all. It was a workroom with a large table and more racks of clothes. At the back of the space, next to a screen door that led to the alley, stood a long rack apparently dedicated entirely to wedding dresses.

Maggie's thoughts went through the list of people who had showed interest in her flapper dress. Harriet had been the most passionate by far. However, it didn't ultimately make sense for Harriet to have taken it. She had wanted it for her collection of vintage wedding dresses, which she proudly displayed in her front window. If she had stolen the dress, she couldn't show it off without others obviously recognizing it. Nonetheless, Maggie was still on alert. Maybe Harriet could have taken the dress simply out of sheer stubbornness. This storage area was as likely a place as any for her dress to be hiding.

Maggie started to take another step into the workroom but was stopped in her tracks by a shrill voice.

"What do you think you're doing?"

10

Maggie stepped back from the workroom abruptly. She turned to face Harriet, who stood with arms crossed, towering over Maggie in her red high heels.

"Oh, it's a workroom," Maggie said, as if just realizing it. "It looked like another changing area. I'm so sorry."

"There are two changing rooms," Harriet said, her voice clipped. She gestured toward the right. "Over there."

"Thanks, Harriet." Maggie shifted the clothing from one arm to the other. "You've got a wonderful turnout today. And the shop is just lovely. You have a real eye for style. And all these clothes? Collecting it all must have taken years."

Harriet softened a bit. "I have to admit that all this started with my own obsession. I have been drawn to classic clothing since I was a girl in the 1950s. Styles changed, but I really didn't change the way I dressed. I was an anomaly for many decades, dressing 'old-fashioned,' as others would say. To me, though, the clothes from many of the earlier decades are timeless. For example, a cardigan—has that ever gone out of style?"

Maggie laughed and held up the cardigan she had chosen to try on. "I hope not."

Harriet smiled tightly. "I always thought I'd end up working in the textile mills in my hometown, but those all closed. It was probably for the best, though, since I ended up as a tailor's assistant. I was just a grunt during the day, but in my free time I designed prom and wedding dresses for local girls. Always classic gowns that really flattered them, inspired by my favorite designer. I even made my own wedding dress."

Maggie glanced at Harriet's ring finger but saw that it was unadorned. "You're married?"

"No, I never found the right man for me. I still have the wedding dress, though. It's part of my collection." She gestured toward the front window.

Maggie followed Harriet's gesture. "You have an impressive array. And styled so beautifully. Is that your entire collection?"

"I saved back a few priceless pieces. I didn't want someone accidentally spilling their latte on them. Or run the risk of having them stolen."

Maggie paused, choosing her words carefully. "Speaking of wedding dresses, I'm afraid I have some bad news. The 1920s wedding dress you were interested in was stolen from my shop yesterday afternoon."

Harriet didn't respond for a few moments. Her voice was stilted when she said, "That's too bad. What happened?"

Maggie explained about how she discovered the dress missing and asked Harriet to keep an ear out for someone trying to sell such a dress. "You have lots of connections in the classic clothing business," Maggie said. "Please let me know if you hear anything."

"Certainly," Harriet said, a hint of dismissiveness in her tone. "Looks like someone is ready to check out. Please excuse me."

Maggie went to the real fitting rooms and tried on the sheath dress, sweater set, and skirt. All were winners, and she was especially delighted by the price tags.

Harriet rang up the sale and thanked her for her purchases. "It was nice chatting with you, Maggie," she said. "I don't have a single friend around town."

"Not for long, I'm sure." Thrown off a little by Harriet's shift in demeanor, Maggie thanked her and took her shopping bag. She was about to say something else, but Harriet's attention had been pulled elsewhere.

Before she left the shop, Maggie walked over to the window display. She wondered if one of the dresses there was the original one Harriet had created for herself, which had never been worn. Then she saw it—a 1950s style that featured a fitted bodice, cap sleeves that nearly fell off the shoulders, and a full, delicately pleated skirt in pure white satin. Maggie looked over at Harriet. The dress would have complemented her tall, willowy figure.

Maggie checked her watch. She had just enough time to drop off her purchases at home and pay a visit to Maxine before her historical society lunch. She walked the few blocks to Sedgwick Manor and let herself in the front door, where Snickers was waiting for her. "Just a quick stopover, buddy," she said, bending to scratch his chin with her free hand.

She closed the door and carried her shopping bag into the master suite closet, Snickers at her heels. As she hung her new purchases, the cat sat at her feet and mewed, looking up toward the high shelf. She followed his gaze to the mysterious torn veil she had draped over her stacked sweaters earlier in the week. "Ah yes, your new toy." In all the excitement, Maggie had nearly forgotten about this damaged veil and the pair of white gold rings hidden in her jewelry box. *I'm glad I didn't display those items in the shop too. If I had, they'd probably be long gone like the dress.*

Maggie let out a dejected breath. It was bad enough that the shop had been broken into, or that at the very least there had been someone there who wasn't supposed to be. *Those eyes.* She shivered a little remembering June's photo of the dress with the eyes peering out from behind the tapestry. As much as ever before, though, Maggie felt as if a piece of her, or a part of her family history at least, had been taken from her, and she was determined to get it back.

With that in mind, Maggie set off to visit Maxine to see

if she could at least determine what she'd been doing driving around town with a large garbage bag yesterday. James had mentioned that Maxine was renting the cottage next door to his friend Everett's house, so she headed in that direction. Maggie was nearly to the corner of Shoreline Drive and Harbor Street when Maxine zipped by on her transporter.

Maggie waved and called, "Maxine!" She thought for sure Maxine had seen her, but the woman continued down the street and wheeled around the corner, either oblivious to or intentionally ignoring Maggie. *Is she avoiding me?*

Hurrying to follow Maxine, Maggie jogged around the corner—and straight into James.

"Whoa, where are you off to?" he asked, brushing a few drops of water off his khaki slacks that had spilled from the bottle in his left hand. He looked professional but casually approachable in a soft blue oxford shirt that was unbuttoned at the collar.

"I'm so sorry, James." Maggie looked down. "Oh no, I spilled your water."

"No big deal. What's the rush?"

"I was hoping to ask Maxine a few questions about where she was yesterday during the burglary." Maggie tucked her hair behind her ears. "I saw her out driving right before I found out the dress had been stolen, and she had an overstuffed black garbage bag with her."

"That sounds a bit suspicious."

Maggie shrugged. "Yes, but it's not like I want to go accusing her of anything. You said she lives near Everett, right?"

"Yes, in a clapboard cottage on the corner. You'll see the patrollers out in front of her garage."

"Thanks, I think she might be headed that way now. Enjoy your water. Or what's left of it, anyway." They said goodbye, and Maggie took off toward Maxine's home.

A short while later, Maggie saw the cottage James had described. She had always admired the charming, one-story house with its siding of sea-weathered gray shingles and its vibrant ocean-blue door. Red and yellow petunias in the front window boxes waved in the light breeze. Two white Adirondack chairs sat next to the front door on a flagstone patio, and in between the chairs was a blue clay pot filled with more petunias. Clusters of daisies were planted at regular intervals next to the home's foundation. The cheerful façade was not quite what Maggie was expecting of a former army MP's home. *Goes to show you can't judge a book by its cover.*

Maggie peeked around the house toward the garage—a detached, gray-shingled building trimmed in white. The large single door was open to reveal six patrollers. A white hand-lettered sign was planted in the yard that read *Lean On Me Tours and Sales*, and another sign close by read *Ring Bell for Service.*

Maggie went back to the house and searched for a doorbell but couldn't find one at first. She looked around the entry and instead saw there was a wrought-iron bell with a clapper hanging to the right side of the front door. She rang the bell and Maxine immediately appeared at the door, opening it wide. She was wearing a black T-shirt tucked into black belted cargo pants, which were in turn tucked into her leather combat boots.

"Oh, it's you." Maxine's tone was flat, so Maggie couldn't quite tell what the woman thought of finding her on her doorstep.

Maggie was about to speak when a police cruiser pulled up in front of Maxine's house. Robert Linton stepped out and approached the front door. "Are you Maxine MacDonald?"

"Yes, why?"

"First of all, we've had some complaints about your vehicles around town, ma'am."

"Complaints? Nonsense." Maxine adjusted her stance as though standing at attention. "As a matter of fact, I was headed to the station today to ask Chief Cole if he'd like to consider outfitting the department with a fleet of my transporters."

"You might want to consider making an appointment first, Ms. MacDonald," Robert said. "In the meantime, I have some questions for you. And this involves you too, Maggie."

Maggie swallowed. "It does?"

Robert nodded and pulled out his notebook. "Ms. MacDonald, there was a burglary at Carriage House Antiques yesterday morning. You were there earlier this week, and it seems you were interested in a wedding dress that was stolen."

"I admit I was at the shop, but I didn't know the dress had gone missing. Go on, sir."

Robert asked Maxine a series of questions about her interest in the dress and whether she thought she had been at all aggressive regarding her desire to purchase the dress. Despite the increasing intensity of the questions, Maxine appeared to remain calm and collected. However, she gave vague answers, saying she had seen the dress and had been slightly interested in it. *That's an understatement.*

"And where were you yesterday morning?" Robert asked.

"I did my laundry, then gave a tour of Somerset Harbor." Maxine's response was terse.

Maggie thought back to seeing Maxine driving around town with the stuffed black garbage bag. *Could that have been her laundry?*

"Do you have a witness that could verify your whereabouts?" Officer Linton asked.

"Not particularly," Maxine said. "A newly married couple were here on their honeymoon and rented two of my personal vehicles. I gave them a tour of the town. I don't have their names."

"You don't write down people's names and contact information when you rent your vehicles? Have them sign a waiver?"

"Of course I do," Maxine said, "but I don't keep the information. You know, there's a lot of liability these days with having people's personal information."

"Where would those records be then?" the officer asked.

"I shred the rental log and then it goes in the trash."

"I'll need to see that trash."

"I'm sorry, sir, but that will be kind of difficult. I get rid of my trash immediately. Clean and orderly is how I keep my quarters."

Robert took a moment, then said very clearly, "Ms. MacDonald, you need to give me that garbage. Now."

Maxine nodded curtly and disappeared inside.

Maggie turned to Robert. "What makes you think Maxine is involved in the burglary?"

"She was seen around that time coming from the direction of Carriage House Antiques with a large plastic bag."

Maggie was taken aback. She hadn't told anyone but James about seeing Maxine with her load, and that had only been a few minutes ago. She knew small-town gossip worked fast, but usually it wasn't that fast. "Who told you that?"

"Aunt Ina. She said she was taking her morning walk when she saw Maxine going up Harbor Street with the bag. That certainly seems very coincidental to me." He looked at Maggie with a smile. "Ina and her police scanner are a match made in heaven. Some days."

"I forgot to tell you yesterday, but I saw her with that bag too."

"You didn't think that information would be important to this investigation? Come on, Maggie, you should know better than that by now," Robert scolded, sounding more like an older brother than an officer of the law.

"Would it help to know that calling you was on my to-do list for the day?"

"I suppose."

Just then, Maxine returned with another black plastic garbage bag, which she tossed with ease to Officer Linton.

"That's my paperwork from yesterday, officer. Fresh out of the receptacle." Maxine once again adopted her military stance.

Robert's face was stony as he said, "Thank you, Ms. MacDonald. I'll be in touch. Good day to you ladies." Robert returned to the police cruiser, got in, and drove away.

Maxine started to go back into the house, then seemed to realize Maggie was still there. "And what was it that you wanted?"

Maggie hesitated. *I came all this way. I suppose I'd better ask her something.* "Well, Maxine, now that my dress has been stolen, I'm even more convinced that it's more special than an ordinary wedding gown. I was wondering if you could tell me a little more about why you think the dress belongs to your family."

"You're wrong about one thing." Maxine's stiff posture seemed to soften a little. "I don't have a family, not really. I was adopted about the time I was born, but the family fell on hard times and had to put me in foster care. I was bounced all over the state of Massachusetts. When I graduated high school, all I wanted was a family, so I joined the army. And now . . ." She paused, looking down the street toward the harbor.

"But that photo you showed me—you said it was your family."

Maxine pulled out her wallet and removed the yellowed newspaper clipping. She gazed at it for what Maggie was sure was the umpteenth time, then handed it to Maggie. "This is the only thing I have from my real mother. I've carried it for more than seventy years, hoping someday I'd know more about who is in it. It's why when I saw that dress the other day, I felt I had to have it. It might be the only connection I could ever have to my birth mother—or anyone else in my family."

Maggie stared at the newsprint photo in her hand. It was weathered and creased, but she could tell that it was almost identical to the photograph she'd found in Evelyn's album. "You might not believe this, but—"

"That's enough boo-hooing," Maxine interrupted gruffly as she snatched the paper back from Maggie's hand. "If you're not here to rent a transporter, I've got other things to do."

Without another word, Maxine stepped back inside the house and closed the door. But she didn't close it soon enough, because something just inside the door caught Maggie's eye: an overstuffed black trash bag tied at the top.

11

Maggie contemplated her conversation with Maxine the entire walk to lunch, wondering why a woman who said she got rid of her garbage immediately still had a tied-up trash bag in her entryway. Thoughts pinged around Maggie's mind right up until she entered The Busy Bean and found her historical society friends at a table in the far corner. Maggie was pleased to see Liz, Fran, Ruth, Ina, and Daisy, who must have taken a break from the kitchen to join the lunch. Daisy motioned to Maggie to indicate that she had a seat saved for her.

Maggie was surprised, however, to see that Harriet was seated between Ruth and Ina. Not only was Harriet not a member of the society, she was also in the midst of her shop's opening day. *What's she doing here?*

"Hi, everyone," Maggie said cheerfully. "Ruth, congratulations on your fifteenth anniversary."

"Hard to believe I've been the society president since I was a teenager," Ruth said with a wink and a wiggle of her gray eyebrows.

Maggie laughed and turned her attention to Harriet. "Harriet, how nice of you to join us. I didn't expect to see you here on your big opening day."

"A girl's gotta eat, you know." Harriet smiled wanly. "I came over to get more scones, and these ladies convinced me to sit down. My assistant, Shelby, is watching the register, though, so I certainly hope no one steals anything while I'm gone. What a terrible thing you had happen, Maggie. Ina here was just filling me in."

Maggie was surprised that Harriet was acting as though Maggie hadn't told her just an hour or two ago that the dress had been stolen. She was not, of course, shocked in the least that the ever-informed Ina had quickly shared everything she knew with the group. "Yes, it was quite upsetting."

Harriet sniffed. "Too bad you hadn't sold that vintage wedding dress to me for my shop display. It might still be around."

Maggie winced at the comment. She really didn't want to get into a discussion about the burglary and missing wedding dress. Instead, she changed the subject. "So, any news on our fall fund-raiser, Ruth?"

"I was just about to ask for ideas, as a matter of fact," Ruth said.

Harriet piped up. "What about a fashion show of several vintage dresses from my shop? We could get the teenage girls from the high school to model them. Girls just love vintage, by the way. And then we could auction them off to raise money."

The ladies around the table broke out into animated discussion about Harriet's suggestion, and Maggie noticed that the woman seemed to glow with pride that her idea was being taken seriously.

"June and I would be happy to help with props," Maggie offered, then did a double take. "Where is June, by the way?"

"She texted and said she got held up at the shop," Fran said from her spot across the table. "Didn't she tell you?"

Maggie's hand automatically went to the back pocket of her jeans to grab her phone and check for text messages, but she found her pocket empty. "Apparently I don't have my phone."

"Where's the last place you had it?" Liz asked.

Maggie thought for a moment and then glanced at Harriet. "A Fine Vintage, actually. I tried on a few outfits this morning and must have left it in the dressing room."

Harriet raised her eyebrows. "I sure hope nobody stole your phone too. You really ought to be more careful with things, Maggie."

The other ladies at the table seemed nonplussed at Harriet's borderline rude statement. Fran spoke up first. "The shop is just across the street next to The Quilt Cupboard. Why don't you go look for it? We'll put in your lunch order for you."

"Lemon chicken is the soup du jour," Daisy said. "It's some of Jack's finest work, if I do say so myself."

"Sounds wonderful," Maggie said. "I'll have that and half a club sandwich. Back in a few."

Maggie dashed out of The Busy Bean and over to A Fine Vintage, which was still buzzing with opening day activity. She went straight to the fitting rooms, which were luckily unoccupied, and searched for her phone. Unfortunately, she didn't see it anywhere. Backing out of the second dressing room, she looked around for a clerk. She didn't see anyone, so she walked over to the third curtained area, the workroom. She poked her head inside to look for Shelby and once again saw the racks of dresses, including the wedding gowns at the back of the room.

Maggie's mind flashed to Harriet's comment about how she hadn't wanted to display her best dresses, and wondered if those were the gowns on the rack in the back room. And if her flapper dress was one of them.

Before she lost her nerve, she approached the long rack, which rested perpendicular to the wall with the screen door on the left side. To its right was a six-foot-high coatrack with wedding veils hanging all around it. Maggie made her way down the rack's right side, which was closest to her, examining the hanging gowns. As she did, she heard a vehicle drive up behind the shop and stop. A car door opened and shut. Was it Harriet? Maggie rolled her eyes at herself. *The woman certainly didn't drive such a short distance to lunch.*

The screen door screeched open and someone entered. Maggie dove behind the rack of veils, not wanting to be caught where she didn't belong.

Maggie heard rustling as the person shuffled through the wedding gowns. She hoped the noise would cover the sound of her pounding heart and her increased respiration.

"Oh, here it is," the person whispered.

Maggie peeked around the veils she was hiding behind and tried to see through the hangers in front of her.

The darkened figure lifted up one of the dresses, walked to the back door, and left without a trace.

After the sound of the vehicle faded, Maggie waited a few moments in case someone else came in. She heard the chatter from inside the store, but all seemed quiet in the alley. Tiptoeing to the screen door, she looked out and then pushed it open slightly. She peeked right, then left, but saw no hint of the vehicle that had just driven away.

Trying to shake off her nerves, Maggie returned to the sales floor and finally located Harriet's assistant at the register. The middle-aged blonde was dressed in a 1960s Chanel suit and had a name tag pinned to her lapel that read *Shelby*.

"Excuse me," Maggie said. "Did anyone find a phone in here earlier?"

"What color case?" Shelby asked.

"It's blue, and the wallpaper on the home screen is of me with a young lady in a graduation cap and gown. My daughter, Emily."

"Yep, we've got it right here." Shelby picked up Maggie's phone from a shelf under the register and handed it to her.

"Thanks so much."

"No problem at all. Please come back soon."

Maggie smiled and left the shop, then jogged across the street to The Busy Bean. Before reentering the café, she ran her hands through her hair and took a deep breath. Smile in place, she walked over to the table, where others were just starting their lunch. Harriet was nowhere to be seen.

"No more Harriet?" Maggie asked as she sat down in front of her lunch.

"As we were placing our orders, she changed her mind about lunch and told us she'd better get back to the shop with the scones," Daisy said, dipping a spoon in her soup. "Her loss. It's such a treat to sit down for lunch in here for a change."

"Yes, speaking of which, let's remember the reason we're all together, shall we?" Liz held up her hands to quiet the conversation around the table. "Ruth, it is with great pride that I present you with this plaque honoring your years of service to the Somerset Harbor Historical Society." Liz handed a wooden plaque bearing a gold faceplate to Ruth as the other ladies applauded.

"Thank you all so much," Ruth said. "It's a privilege to be a keeper of our town's history."

"We also had a bit of fun putting this together for you," Fran said, offering Ruth a glittery silver gift bag with pink tissue paper coming out of the top.

Ruth laughed with delight as she pulled a scrapbook from the bag.

"We've had a lot of fund-raisers and events over the years," Fran continued. "And none of them would have happened without you."

The ladies spent the next half hour giggling and reminiscing over photos of themed fund-raisers they had participated in through the years. As lunch wound down, Ina insisted that they all pose for a photograph together. "For my column," she said. "Thaddeus says I've been giving him so much material, he might even give me my own blug."

"You mean 'blog,' Ina?" Daisy asked. "You know, word around town is that you might have another event coming up that'd be just perfect for your social column. Or your blog."

"Never you mind that, Daisy," Ina said as she put her camera back in her fanny pack. "Today is about Ruth."

"Yes, and thank you all so much for the wonderful celebration," Ruth said. "What thoughtful friends I have. And now I'd best be getting back to the museum we're all so very fond of."

The ladies all gathered their belongings. Each tried to pay her share, but Daisy waved off their offers. "Ruth's party is on me."

Everyone thanked Daisy and left the café. Ina strode briskly toward her home to listen to her police scanner, Fran crossed the street to go back to The Quilt Cupboard, and Ruth and Liz said they were headed back toward Old Faith Chapel. "Where are you off to, Maggie?" Liz asked.

Maggie thought about her day's to-do list for a moment. "I thought I might go over to the library. Maura's niece, Magenta, offered to do some part-time work for me while she's in town this summer. I wanted to talk through the details with Maura a bit. Poor girl, her parents are getting a divorce, and I think she's a little at loose ends."

"Magenta?" Liz asked. "She must have a colorful personality."

Maggie smiled. "Yes, I think it's a self-proclaimed nickname. Anyway, I'll walk with you two since you're going in that direction."

They strolled around the corner and up the street. Halfway up the block, they approached a trio of ten- or eleven-year-old boys. The two taller ones were playing keep-away with something small, while a shorter redheaded boy was trying to intercept the item being tossed.

"Hello, young men," Ruth said as they passed the boys. "No school today?"

All three boys stopped what they were doing, and one of the taller ones held the item in his hand.

"It's a half day, Mrs. Harper," the redhead explained.

Ruth looked each boy in the eyes, then said, "And what, may I ask, are you doing with my key?"

"Your key?" The boy who held the keep-away object in his hand sounded nervous.

"Yes, Mr. Griffin, the key to the attic of the historical society." Ruth stared him down. "It seems to have gone missing the other day. And it seems to have reappeared in your hand." She held out her hand, palm up. "If you return it to me now, I won't have to inform your mother."

In an instant, the boy placed the key in Ruth's hand. All three raced off and disappeared around the corner.

"What was that all about?" Liz asked.

Ruth's stony face broke into a smile as she examined the key, then pocketed it. "Maggie got stuck in the attic of the society building the other day while she was going through old records. Those boys were part of the school group that came into the museum the day before, and when they left, this key seems to have gone with them."

Maggie laughed. "Glad to know it was nothing more than juvenile hijinks and humidity. I was trying not to let my imagination get the best of me."

"Often the simplest explanation is the true one," Ruth said as they continued walking.

Maggie said goodbye to her friends when they all reached the sidewalk in front of the library, where young moms and toddlers were parading out the front door. *Good timing. Story time is over, so Maura should be free.*

As Maggie entered, she saw Maura vacuuming the colorfully carpeted corner in the children's section. She waved, and Maura indicated that she would be right with her. As Maggie walked to the counter, Magenta turned her lips up slightly but then headed to the back with a large stack of books in her arms, presumably to reshelve them.

At the counter, Pearl stood hunched over the computer again.

She wore another black T-shirt, this time bearing a graphic that read, *I am no bird; and no net ensnares me; I am a free human being with an independent will.* —*Charlotte Brontë*, Jane Eyre.

"Hi, Pearl," Maggie said. "Nice shirt."

Pearl's gaze flitted from the screen to Maggie and back again. "Have you finished *Jane Eyre*?"

"No, I'm embarrassed to say I haven't started it yet."

"Too busy looking for your wedding dress." Pearl's tone of voice presented that as a statement rather than a question.

"How did you hear about that?" Maggie asked.

Pearl continued to stare at the computer. "You learn a lot when you listen rather than speak."

"You sure hit the nail on the head there, Pearl."

Pearl's brow furrowed. "I'm not very handy around the house."

Maggie fought back a smile. She was starting to find Pearl's literal interpretation of things more endearing than off-putting.

"Can I help you, Maggie?" Magenta had appeared at her elbow.

"Hi, Magenta. I actually came to settle things with your aunt about you working for me. You're not too busy, are you?"

"I was just shelving books," Magenta said. "Straightening things. People are so ridiculous, putting books in the wrong places or just leaving them anywhere."

"How goes the computer training?"

Magenta shrugged. "I think Aunt Maura has decided I'm a hopeless cause. Good thing she has Pearl here." The girl nodded at Pearl, whom Maggie assumed was listening despite the fact that she was still staring intently at her monitor. "She and my aunt have moved on from creating an online catalog to joining social media. Pearl said she would—and I'm quoting her—'blitz the Internet with everything there is to know about the Somerset Harbor Library.' She said it was about time we moved into the twenty-first century."

"It sounds like everyone is using their God-given talents, at least," Maggie said.

Magenta shrugged again. "Any word on the missing wedding dress?"

Maggie was taken aback. "You've heard about that too? Small-town gossip is certainly a force to be reckoned with."

"No, I just read it in the newspaper," Magenta said. "Come here—I'll show you." Magenta led Maggie to the reading area of comfy chairs and side tables. She handed the latest issue of *The Somerset Harbor Herald* to Maggie. The front page headline read, Local Shop Burglarized: Wedding Dress Stolen.

Maggie skimmed the article, which was accompanied by a photograph of the window display as it had looked a few days earlier, before the dress was stolen. Apparently upgraded from society columnist, Ina had a front-page byline and photo credit. *It must have been a slow news day in Somerset Harbor.*

"I only read it because I heard you say something about a wedding dress the other day," Magenta said, "and I knew you were looking for books on vintage fashion. I hope you get your dress back."

Just then, Maura approached Maggie and Magenta. "I don't know why they're making such a fuss about your dress," she said, pointing to the newspaper. "No offense, Maggie, but it's not like it's the Hope Diamond or anything."

"Agreed," Maggie said. "It's important to me personally, but it doesn't seem to be fitting for front-page news."

Maggie started to set the newspaper back, but Magenta intercepted it, folded it carefully, and placed it on the table in alignment with a handful of magazines. "Um, Maggie?" she said timidly.

"Yes?"

Magenta seemed to hesitate, then she got a determined look on her face and said, "I think I saw something yesterday.

Something suspicious. Have you been to that new vintage clothing store?"

"I have," Maggie said. "It's lovely. I stopped by the opening day reception just this morning."

"Well, last night, I was walking around town scoping things out."

"The O'Brien household isn't exciting enough for a teenager, I'm afraid," Maura said good-naturedly.

"Oh, it's not that, Aunt Maura. I just figure if I'm going to be here all summer, I might as well know my way around. Anyway, I decided to go down the alley behind the shops—I like dark, creepy kinds of places. While I was walking, I noticed a tall lady taking clothes out of her car. It was a vintage car."

"A 1957 Chevrolet?" Maggie asked.

"I don't know," Magenta said. "It was just old. The lady was taking clothes out of her car and into the back door of that shop. I didn't think much of it. But just as I was walking by, I saw her carry a white dress in through that door."

"Was it a big poufy wedding gown or more like a cocktail dress?" Maura asked. "Maggie made it sound like her dress wasn't a fancy princess type."

"All I really saw was a big pile of white fabric, but it was sparkling in the moonlight, so I figured it was a wedding dress."

Maggie looked Magenta straight in the eye. "Do you think it might have been a flapper-style dress?"

Magenta shrugged her shoulders. "I really don't know. I don't want to say I saw something when I'm not sure. But it seems like a no-brainer to me. She sells vintage wedding dresses. You get one stolen. Perfectly logical."

Maggie didn't want to say that she'd actually been in the back workroom of A Fine Vintage earlier that afternoon. Instead, she said, "It is logical from one standpoint, but Harriet collects wedding dresses, so if it was her and her car, she could have been carrying any wedding dress. Not necessarily mine. She has a large selection of them for people to buy."

"Besides," Maura interjected, "she certainly wouldn't keep the dress in her shop where anyone could find it, would she? I'm not sure how I feel about you tossing around accusations, young lady."

"Sorry, Aunt Maura." Magenta looked contrite. "I thought I should say something, just in case it might help."

"And I appreciate it, Magenta," Maggie said. "I'd much rather you said something than kept it to yourself if it might have been important. You're very good at being helpful."

"Speaking of which," Maura said, "do you still want her to work for you, Maggie?"

"Yes, definitely. I thought she could start out by organizing the Sedgwick Manor library. Do you think you could spare her half a day here and there?"

"I think it's a wonderful idea," Maura said. "She's a whiz with organizing, especially books."

"Can you start tomorrow?" Maggie asked, turning to the teenager. "Maybe one o'clock?"

Maura and Magenta both agreed, and Maggie said goodbye. On her way out, Maggie noticed that Pearl wasn't at the checkout counter. *I guess even computer geniuses need to take a break every so often.*

Thinking about what Magenta had said about her experiences behind A Fine Vintage the previous night, Maggie decided to detour down the alley. As she turned into the narrow passage lined with the backs of brick buildings, Maggie noticed someone with a long gray braid in a long black skirt just leaving the alley on the other side of the block. Pearl.

And she was carrying a dress bag with white fabric peeking out from the bottom.

12

Maggie took off at a jog. *Why would Pearl be leaving the alley with a dress bag?* When Maggie got to Harbor Street, she looked left up the hill and right toward the harbor, but there was no sign of Pearl. Was the older woman headed home? Maggie trotted up the hill toward the neighborhood where Ina and Pearl lived.

Maggie slowed to a walk as she passed Ina's house. *The last thing I need is for the Herald's new reporter to think I'm chasing someone.*

"Where are you off to, Maggie?" Ina stepped out onto the porch of her white clapboard home and waved. She was wearing a red gingham apron that matched her red front door. "Want a homemade energy bar? I use my dehydrated veggies from my own garden."

"No thanks, Ina. I'm still full from lunch." Maggie gave up her pursuit of Pearl and walked over to chat with Ina. "When did you find time to make energy bars with your new journalism career?"

"Sounds like you saw the article in the *Herald*."

"I did, just now. Great job with the byline and all." Maggie glanced up the street. "Ina, I was actually looking for someone—a new volunteer at the library. I heard she lives near you."

"Which one? Pearl or Mary Catherine, who prefers to be known as Magenta?" Ina sounded as though she appreciated the young girl's individualism.

"Pearl. I thought I saw her coming this way."

"She did, just a minute ago. She's renting the cottage next to the B&B the next block up. It's the one to the right, not behind it."

Maggie knew the place immediately. "Thank you, Ina."

"No problem. And stop by on your way home if you change your mind about the energy bars."

Ina retreated into the house, and Maggie set off toward the cottage Ina had directed her to. When she came to the corner, she turned right and saw Pearl's rental right away. It looked much like Ina's house along with several others in the area. The façade had a similar bay window, and there were half a dozen stairs leading up to a seafoam-green door. Hanging around the bay window were flower boxes—but they were empty. Perhaps Pearl didn't have a green thumb. *She'd certainly tell me that her thumb is flesh-toned, not green.*

Maggie walked up the steps and knocked at the door. No response. Then she knocked again. After half a minute of waiting, Maggie saw a curtain stir in the nearby bay window. Maggie knocked one more time, but there was no answer.

Maggie sighed and descended the steps. On the sidewalk, she stopped to think. She now had reason to suspect Maxine, Harriet, and Pearl of having her wedding dress, but her evidence was entirely circumstantial. She had seen Maxine with an overstuffed garbage bag, Magenta had mentioned seeing someone fitting Harriet's description with a wedding gown outside her shop, and now Pearl had disappeared into her own home with a dress bag. *Maybe I should get them all in a room together and see what happens.* Maggie almost laughed at the idea of the three very different women socializing.

Her thoughts kept returning to the black garbage bag she'd seen resting just inside Maxine's front door. True, it could be anything. The woman had given Officer Linton shredded paperwork tied up in the same type of bag, after all. But Maggie couldn't help but think that she could at least rule Maxine out if she could figure out what was inside the bag she had seen.

She contemplated how abruptly her last visit to Maxine's house had ended. Then she realized that if she wanted to get in the woman's good graces and hoped to get inside the house, she just might have to take one of those patrollers for a test drive after all.

With renewed determination, Maggie walked the few blocks to Maxine's house. The front door stood open, presumably to let the breezes blow through and cool the house down. Maggie wondered if she might be able to peek inside, but then she saw Maxine storming toward her from the direction of the garage.

"I told you I don't have time to—" Maxine started to speak, but Maggie held up a hand to quiet her.

"I'd actually like to try out one of your patrollers. Do you have time to show me?"

Maxine seemed confused for a moment, then gruffly said, "I suppose I do. It's thirty dollars an hour, but I'll give you a deal for twenty."

"Thanks, Maxine. First, though, I've been running around town all day doing errands, and . . . I hate to ask, but would it be possible for me to use your powder room?"

"Certainly," Maxine said, pointing behind the garage. "This way."

Maggie hesitated. This was not what she had in mind.

"I have rented a facility for situations such as this," Maxine said. "You'll find it behind the garage."

"Thank you," Maggie said, heading in that direction. Sure enough, there was the familiar-looking boxy structure ubiquitous at outdoor events. Maggie waited a couple of minutes behind the garage, then returned to Maxine, whose right leg now was jiggling with impatience.

"Ready now?" Maxine asked.

"There's just one more thing. Since I've been running around town all day doing all those errands I mentioned earlier,

I also wondered if it would be too much trouble for me to get a glass of water. It certainly turned warm today, didn't it?" Maggie pushed the sleeves of her cardigan up on her forearms.

"I've thought of that too." Maxine walked over to a blue-and-white plastic ice chest sitting in the shade of the garage. She opened it and pulled out a dripping bottle of water and handed it to Maggie. "That will be one dollar." She held out her hand.

Maggie pulled out her wallet and removed a twenty-dollar bill and a single. "That's for the rental and the water. It looks as though you've thought of everything, Maxine." Maggie took a long drink out of the bottle, thinking. "You know, I've always admired this cute house. And you've done such a nice job with the flowers out front. I especially love the daisies. I bet it's charming inside." She took another sip, waiting for a response.

"Yes, it'll do," Maxine said. "It's enough for me. Look, are you ready for this ride or not? I've got another customer coming in less than an hour. Maybe you want to come back another day."

"No," Maggie said, "I'm just making conversation here while I get a little drink."

At that moment Maxine's cell phone rang, and she took the phone out of her back pocket and answered it. "Hello? Yes, I do." Then she turned to Maggie. "I've got to take this call. I'll be back in a couple minutes." And with that she walked behind the garage.

Maggie could hear Maxine talking to someone but couldn't make out anything. Maybe she could just peek in the front door and see if the bag was even where it had been earlier today. Maggie stepped sideways to the house, keeping an eye on the back of the garage to make sure Maxine wasn't headed back, then walked up the few steps to the open front door. She peered in.

The house was indeed small, with just one great room downstairs and a stairway that presumably led to a bedroom under the eaves of the roof. The furnishings were simple. Maggie saw a brown suede recliner, a small plaid sofa, and a television on an empty bookshelf in the living area, and a simple, square wooden table and two chairs in the kitchen. There was no bag in the small entry area as there had been earlier. However, she did spy two large plastic bags sitting in a far corner of the kitchen.

"Ahem." Maxine cleared her throat.

Maggie turned around and started to speak, but Maxine cut her off.

"Maggie, you've been hinting around at trying to see my house since you've been here," Maxine said. "Here it is. Not much to it, but it's enough for me. Have you satisfied your curiosity now? If so, let's get this patroller on the road, with you on it."

Maggie decided that saying nothing was probably best. She followed Maxine to the garage, signed a waiver, and listened intently to instructions about operating the patroller. She watched closely as Maxine demonstrated it, hoping she wouldn't end up in the grass like Ina.

After the demonstration, Maggie put on the helmet Maxine handed her and climbed on. Maxine started it up, and, with a slight lean, Maggie was turning around and headed out onto the street.

One thing Maggie had not taken into consideration was the fact that half of Somerset Harbor's streets were either up or down, and now she was going down Harbor Street. Although she was probably traveling under twelve miles per hour—Maggie was afraid to take her eyes off the road to check the speedometer—this was reminding her of her nightmare when she flew off the cliff.

Maggie shook off the memory of her bad dream and focused on learning to maneuver the vehicle. She figured out how to do enough of a lean back to slow the patroller—but not so much as to make it go backward and dump her. After a few minutes cruising down one street and up another, Maggie had a sense of how to control the vehicle. She was having considerably more fun than she had expected, and she made a mental note to get business cards from Maxine to put out with the other tourism pamphlets she had available at Carriage House Antiques.

After a loop through the business district, around past the police station, and then back up and in front of the municipal building, she felt confident enough to head a little farther. Maybe she could try again at Pearl's house to see if she would answer.

However, as Maggie approached Pearl's cottage, the retired librarian was walking in the opposite direction toward town. *Maybe I could just slip inside . . .* But Maggie chided herself for even thinking such a thing, especially when she had just gotten in trouble with Maxine for just looking into her home from the front door. Besides, she had had others break into her home before and knew how violating it felt. She drove on.

As Maggie tooled around town, her mind wandered, but her thoughts continually returned to the strange notion she'd had earlier to get Harriet, Pearl, and Maxine in a room together, and maybe Magenta too. All the women were new to Somerset Harbor, and each had a prickly way about her that Maggie thought could merely be due to a lack of friends in town. Then again, it could also be due to a guilty conscience. *If I invited them over, would they come?* Maggie could start by asking her friends from the historical society to Sedgwick Manor for lunch, then find ways to entice the other women. Two had businesses to promote, and maybe Maura, Magenta, and Pearl could come together on a break from the library. Even if none of Somerset Harbor's most recent inhabitants showed up, at least Maggie would still have her friends there.

By the time Maggie turned into Maxine's driveway, a plan had formed in her mind. As she slowed down, she saw a young couple standing near the garage, finishing up their paperwork.

Maggie rolled slowly to a stop. She dismounted and unhooked the helmet, then rested it on top of the patroller. "That was really fun, Maxine. Do you have any extra business cards that I could keep at Carriage House Antiques? Tourists stop there a lot, and I'd be happy to recommend they give you a call."

Maxine reached into her pocket and handed a dozen or so cards to Maggie.

As she tucked the business cards in her purse, Maggie leaned in and said quietly, "And I'm sorry about . . . earlier. You have a lovely home."

Maxine gave her a stern look. "When I was in the army, I learned to follow the rules. I follow the rules. You should too." And then she went back to the garage to get the Segways the couple had rented.

As she walked down the driveway toward the sidewalk, Maggie heard the couple talk animatedly about how fun their tour would be, teasing each other about who would fall off first. Smiling at their playfulness, Maggie thought about how much joy Maxine might bring to Somerset Harbor with her adventurous new business. And she hoped that Maxine was not the person who stole her wedding dress.

As she walked up the sidewalk to Sedgwick Manor, it seemed that something more was there than her weekly copy of *The Somerset Harbor Herald*. A simple white envelope was propped against the base of the door. She picked it up and opened it. Inside there wasn't a letter—it was a note card with a message written in all capital letters:

THE DRESS IS STILL IN TOWN.

13

Maggie examined the note. She couldn't place the handwriting, which was almost artistically fashioned with its carefully printed capital letters. She sniffed the card, thinking stationery could smell like the person who sent it, and different homes have different scents that permeate everything in the house. The cardstock smelled simply of paper, clean and sanitary, as though it had come right from the store. *Maybe it did.*

In any case, it was time to call Officer Linton. Maggie dialed his cell phone and let herself into the house. He picked up on the third ring.

"Robert, I just found a note on my doorstep—a white card that says, 'The dress is still in town.'"

"You don't happen to recognize the handwriting, do you?"

"No," Maggie said. "It's just block letters. It seems as though someone was trying to disguise the handwriting."

"Do your best to not leave additional fingerprints on it," Robert advised. "Slip it into a clean plastic bag, and drop it by the station as soon as you can." He paused for a moment. "And Maggie, take care. This note tells me that someone other than your burglar could know who took the dress, and the complication concerns me."

"I can bring it by tomorrow morning if that works for you," Maggie said. "And I'll be careful. Anything new to report on the investigation?"

"I talked with everyone I could track down who shopped in the store this week, and they can all account for their whereabouts during the burglary," he said. "I won't lie to you, Maggie. I'm having a dickens of a time trying to piece together Maxine's shredded paperwork. I think it's all mixed up with credit card offers and other junk she got in the mail that day."

"Sounds pretty rough, Robert. Maybe Nora and Bobby can help?"

"Nah," he said. "Nora hates it when I bring work home. And she'd definitely hate it if the work I brought home was actual trash."

With a chuckle, Maggie wished him a good evening and hung up. As she disconnected the call, she realized that the remaining item on her to-do list was to call Emily and check in. As she fed Snickers his dinner, she dialed her daughter.

"Hi, Mom." Emily sounded exhausted.

"Hey sweetie, everything okay?"

"It's fine. I'm just super tired from work and getting things squared away with the apartment. I got my lease signed the other day, but since then I've been trying to set up appointments with the utility companies between shifts. I can't wait to be settled in."

"Sounds like a lot, but I know you can handle it. Let me know if I can help in any way. And I can't wait to see this new place."

"The sooner the better," Emily said. "I need your help decorating."

Maggie smiled, appreciating that her adult daughter still valued her input. "I've got some great pieces in the shop I think will be perfect for you. I'll send some photos next time I get a chance."

"Awesome. Thanks, Mom. Speaking of the shop, have you learned anything about that 1920s dress you sent me a photo of the other day? I've been wondering about it."

Maggie sighed. "Oh, Emily. I don't even know where to start."

"How about the beginning? I need a good story while I eat my dinner."

"Careful what you wish for," Maggie said, then told Emily about how she found the dress and displayed it in Carriage House Antiques. She mentioned the contest she and June had come up with to try and ferret out its history and connection to Sedgwick Manor. Then Maggie described the instant interest the dress had created. "There are two newcomers to town, Maxine and Harriet, who were rather intimidating in their requests. Harriet wanted the dress for her wedding gown collection, which she has in the window of her new vintage clothing store. Maxine insisted the dress was a family heirloom—she even showed me a picture."

"Wow, this sounds crazy, Mom."

"Yeah, but what's even crazier is that I found almost the same photo in one of Aunt Evelyn's albums. I haven't had a chance to talk to Maxine about it yet though."

"Did you find any information about the dress, like if it was Aunt Evelyn's or not? It doesn't really seem like her style, does it?"

"No," Maggie said, "I think it would be from the generation before hers, or even longer. Did I mention the matching veil?"

"I bet that's lovely, Mom. Describe it for me."

Maggie told her about the veil and rings, then took a deep breath. "What's truly going to blow your mind is that the dress was stolen."

"No way! What happened?"

Maggie gave her the details of the burglary and the investigation, both Robert's work and her own casual sleuthing.

"Mom, that's horrible. Did the thief take the veil and the rings too?"

"Thankfully I still have those—I'm just keeping them out of sight for the time being. I'll take a photo of the veil and text it to you. Hang on." Maggie walked to her bedroom, got the veil from her closet, laid it out on her bed, and took a photo, which she immediately texted to Emily. "Hi, you there?"

"Yes, Mom. The veil is absolutely gorgeous."

"It matches the dress perfectly. Except for one thing."

"What's that?"

"Take another look at the photo. The veil is torn in half, from the bottom to the top."

"You're kidding. That sounds just like what happened in *Jane Eyre*, one of my favorite novels we read in English class senior year of high school."

"James said the same thing. He wouldn't spill any details of the story, though, so I have to read it for myself. I checked the book out of the library, and I hope to finally crack it open tonight. But you could tell me what the torn veil thing is all about. Please?"

Emily laughed. "It would be so far-fetched if your torn veil had anything to do with the story in the novel. But you're such a romantic, Mom—you love suspenseful mysteries and happy endings—I bet you won't be able to put that book down."

Their conversation continued another half an hour. Maggie turned on her speakerphone so she could prepare herself a chicken stir-fry for dinner. She listened raptly as Emily talked about how ragged she felt after long shifts, but in the same breath she talked about how gratifying her work was and how much she loved the staff at the hospital. Sometimes, she said, the patients and their families were challenging, a bit grouchy, but she tried to look beneath the surface and imagine the struggles they were having. "They're right when they say you can't judge a book by its cover, you know. I remember how it felt when Dad died, and I try to be empathetic. It can be hard while trying to do my job, but I like to think I'm getting a little better every day. And I can see how my work helps people feel better."

"I'm really proud of you," Maggie said, feeling a sudden wave of emotion.

"Thanks, Mom. Sorry, but I need to go. I'm starting another shift in half an hour."

"Okay, honey. Take care. I love you."

"Love you too." And with that, Emily was gone, back to her new life in her new town.

Maggie replaced her phone in her pocket, then poured her stir-fry onto a plate and grabbed silverware and a glass of water. She sat down with her dinner and *Jane Eyre*. She opened the front cover and turned to the first chapter. "There was no possibility of taking a walk that day . . ."

Maggie was riveted to Jane from the first pages—an orphaned girl whose aunt abused her and forced her to go to a boarding school, where she was malnourished and mistreated. Maggie couldn't put the book down as she followed Jane's personal journey to become a teacher at Lowood School—*Isn't that an appropriate name?*—and then a governess for a mysterious master, Mr. Edward Rochester. Slowly Jane found herself drawn to her standoffish master, as he was to her.

When Maggie glanced up at the clock, she realized that time had slipped by at an alarming rate since she started reading. It took effort to tear herself away from the trials of young Jane, but she did. She tidied up the kitchen, all the while thinking about what Emily had said. *You can't judge a book by its cover.* The statement felt especially apropos when it came to Harriet, Pearl, Maxine, and Magenta. Were these odd ducks acting so suspicious around Maggie simply because they were new to town and unsure of themselves? Or had one of them stolen the dress? With that in mind, she continued her mental planning to invite her friends and the Somerset Harbor newbies to lunch on Saturday.

While getting ready for bed, Maggie looked at the veil, still draped across her quilt. How could a veil become torn? It wasn't long enough for someone to step on and rip. Perhaps it had gotten caught in a car door, or stuck on a doorjamb. Maggie shrugged. The veil looked as though it had been ripped from the bottom to the top on purpose. Maybe the love went wrong. Maybe the groom skipped out. Maybe someone was simply jealous.

She picked the veil up by the headpiece and admired the beautiful creation. Off-white satin and lace were layered one over the other in the same scalloped design as the dress. She loved the white sequined flower off to the side, characteristic of the flapper style of the 1920s. *Any woman would feel beautiful wearing this.*

On a whim, Maggie put it on, then walked into the adjacent bathroom to look in the mirror. She chuckled. She looked a bit haggard after her day tromping around Somerset Harbor. She grabbed a hand mirror, then swiveled around to see what the veil looked like from the back. The tear was noticeable, at least to her.

Maggie got her phone out of her pocket and took a photo of herself in the mirror, laughing. *I'm like one of those teenagers, taking pictures of themselves in the mirror all the time. What would Emily think?* Realizing her daughter would probably get a good laugh, Maggie texted her the photo.

Maggie removed the veil and hung it on a hanger, then set it over the side of her closet door. Finding the dress and learning the history of it and the secret behind the torn veil somehow seemed even more important now. Evelyn had saved them for a reason. She just needed to figure out what.

Maggie had brought her copy of *Jane Eyre* into the bedroom with her and set it by her favorite chair in the sitting area.

She was tired from her long day, but she couldn't resist reading just a little more . . .

Even as the clock ticked toward midnight, Maggie kept reading, only to find out that there was a mystery in the attic in Thornfield, the name of the remote yet grand estate home of Mr. Rochester. And then there was an engagement and a planned wedding, but Jane found the wedding veil ripped from the bottom to the top, and the wedding ceremony never happened.

Ah, there's the connection. The canceled wedding. An unused wedding dress. A torn veil.

Maggie felt her eyes closing. She wanted to keep reading, but she just couldn't. She set the book down and headed for bed.

As she fell asleep, one thought kept coming to mind. Could the ripped veil that was now hanging on Maggie's closet door have had the same kind of odd history as that told in *Jane Eyre*? If so, there was another place she needed to investigate.

The Sedgwick Manor attic.

14

Maggie went to the police station first thing the next morning. The station's main room was simple—a counter and an open area with desks for the various officers. Beyond the main room, Maggie could see Chief Cole's office and the area leading to the holding cells.

Robert Linton stood at the front counter, where he appeared to be sorting the shredded paper that Maggie assumed was Maxine's garbage. "You're out early, Maggie. Is that the note you received yesterday?"

Maggie handed him the bag containing the card and envelope. "It's rather curious, don't you think?"

Officer Linton read the note: "'The dress is still in town.' Yes, curious is one way to put it. What's your take on it?"

"It could mean that someone knows who stole the dress. But it could be an indication that whoever stole it intends to return it. As though they were just, I don't know, borrowing the dress? It's a stretch, but I'm trying to remain hopeful. What do you think?"

The officer looked from the note to Maggie. "The letter is written by someone who knows you—someone who knows you're concerned about the dress, someone who understands that it has significance to you personally. That's my hunch. Best-case scenario is that it's returned to you soon."

"I hope so, Robert," Maggie said. "Can fingerprints be done on paper?"

"Paper is commonly tested for fingerprints in forensics, but it is challenging to make them visible," he said. "Half the time it

works, so I could give it a try. Wouldn't mind a break, frankly."
He gestured to the mess of shredded paper in front of him.

"So it's a piece of work," Maggie joked, then laughed along with Robert. "Whatever the outcome of the case, I want to let you know that I appreciate everything you've done to help me."

"You're very welcome, Maggie, though I probably shouldn't say that until I actually have something to show for my troubles," he said. "Just hold on a sec and I'll make you a copy of the note."

Robert used the nearby copy machine to duplicate the note, then handed the copy to Maggie. "Maybe something will come to you as you look at it a few more times."

Maggie folded the paper and put it into her pocket. After saying goodbye, she left the station and decided she'd go to The Busy Bean for a cup of coffee and a dose of Daisy's trademark sunshine.

Daisy greeted her with just that courtesy of a wide smile. "Good morning, Maggie. What'll it be?"

Maggie walked up to the counter where Daisy stood. "First things first. Would you like to come to lunch at my house tomorrow?"

"Two lunches with you in one week?" Daisy pretended to fan herself. "How lucky can a girl get? What's the occasion?"

"Nothing in particular. I just feel like being social," Maggie said. "I'm going to ask Ruth, Ina, Liz, Fran, and June to come, of course. I also thought I'd invite some of the new ladies in town, like Harriet Hamstead and Maxine MacDonald, and the new library volunteer, Pearl Winters."

"You mean the ones who might have stolen your dress?" Daisy put a hand to her mouth and stepped back. "Not that I'd ever think such a thing."

Maggie chided Daisy with a playful *tsk-tsk*. "I don't know where you get your information."

"You know I have my sources, but this one starts with an *I* and ends with a *nuh*."

"I should have figured. I honestly don't know what to think. But I do know that I want you to whip up something special for dessert."

"Special is my specialty," Daisy said, and she got out an order form she used for catering. "How about individual chocolate cups filled with chocolate mousse and topped with real whipped cream? And maybe chocolate shavings on top for good measure."

"I'll take two dozen," Maggie said.

"I could go for two dozen myself." James had appeared at the counter without Maggie realizing it.

Daisy looked pointedly at his running clothes. "Carb loading after your run, James?"

He laughed. "I suppose it might defeat the purpose. I guess I'll have to settle for a cup of Jamaican blend to go."

"Same for you, Maggie?" Daisy raised her eyebrows.

"Yes please, and one for June."

"Coming right up, you two." Daisy filled three to-go cups and returned in record time. As she was ringing up Maggie's coffee and special order, she said, "I'll have these ready first thing tomorrow morning."

"Thanks, Daisy," Maggie said, putting away her wallet and grabbing the cardboard carrier holding two cups of coffee. "You're a dear."

"So I hear. Sometimes, at least." Daisy winked. "You two enjoy your day." With a wave, Daisy went to go refill coffee for the breakfast crowd.

"So what are the chocolate desserts for?" James asked, leading Maggie away from the front counter gently by the elbow. "I assume they aren't your breakfast today."

"I'm having a lunch at my house tomorrow. Want to come?"

James held the door open and Maggie stepped out onto the sidewalk with him right behind her. "I'd love to, but Mother and I are going to visit some family friends for lunch. Technically it's work and pleasure for me since they have an old Chesterfield tufted sofa they want advice on restoring. Who all is coming?"

"Just Daisy so far, but I'm planning to invite the rest of the usual crew. I also think I'm going to see if some of the new faces in town would like to join us. Maybe they'd even be interested in joining the historical society or helping with some upcoming fund-raisers."

"Or maybe you'll be able to figure out which one of them stole your dress?" James wiggled his finger at her.

"Touché. You know me too well." Maggie glanced across the street and caught sight of A Fine Vintage. It wasn't quite ten o'clock, and Harriet's chalkboard sign wasn't out front yet. She looked at James. "I got a note yesterday about the dress. It kind of spooked me at first but sort of reassured me at the same time."

James leaned toward her. "What did it say?"

Maggie got the copy of the note out of her pocket and handed it to him.

James mouthed the words as he read.

"Sort of odd, don't you think?" Maggie asked.

"No signature, just that one line in all capital letters. Carefully done, it seems, so as to disguise the handwriting." James handed the note back to Maggie, who folded it and put it back in her pocket. "And how did you get it? By mail?"

"No, it was sitting on my doorstep when I got home late yesterday afternoon."

"Strange," James said. "I wonder if anyone in the area might have seen the person coming or going."

"I hadn't even thought of that. I'll ask June. Speaking of which, I'd better get to the shop before her coffee gets cold."

A few minutes later, Maggie found June just unlocking the front door of the antiques shop for the day. "Good morning, June. I brought you a coffee."

"You sure know the way to my heart," June said, taking her cup and holding the door open for Maggie as she entered. "Any news from Robert about the dress?"

"Not necessarily from Robert, but there's this." Maggie handed June the note. "This was sitting on my doorstep late yesterday afternoon. Did you see anyone coming or going from the manor?"

"Sorry, I didn't see anyone. It was pretty busy here yesterday." June examined the note carefully. "I have to say, that handwriting looks familiar for some reason, even though it looks forced or practiced—you know, not natural. I wish I could place it."

"I felt that way too when I first saw it. Hopefully it'll come to us soon." Maggie took a sip of her coffee and then sighed. "I won't lie, I am a bit frustrated with all this. The dress just had—still has—a draw for me. It's as though it has a purpose yet to be discovered. Does that make sense?"

June smirked. "Maybe you're supposed to wear it?"

Maggie rolled her eyes. "Cute."

"What about Emily? She's bound to get married some day in the not-too-distant future."

"She might be a little busy for romance these days." Maggie summarized some of the highlights of her conversation with Emily. "I'm so proud of her. And she inspired me to have a luncheon tomorrow. I know it's short notice, but maybe you could close the shop for an hour and come over?"

"Wouldn't miss it," June said. "Let me know if I can help with prep at all."

"For now, I just need to work on inviting everyone. I'm going to wander over to A Fine Vintage first."

"A Fine Vintage? You're inviting Harriet?"

"I know she rubbed us both the wrong way at first, but I got to thinking that she's new in town, and maybe she just needs to make some friends."

"You've got a good heart, Maggie." June took another sip of her coffee.

"I hope you feel the same way when you find out I'm inviting Maxine MacDonald and Maura's two new library volunteers as well."

"I hadn't realized how many new retirement-age residents Somerset Harbor had gotten recently," June said. "Did the city council start up an ad campaign we didn't know about?"

Chuckling, Maggie said, "Could be."

"Speaking of retirees, my parents were really excited to hear you'd come watch them compete at the Dancing With the Seniors contest tonight. We're still on, right?"

"Wouldn't miss it."

"They'll be thrilled to see you. I asked Mom if anyone else we know is competing, but she wouldn't say."

"Part of the fun could be not knowing." Maggie checked the time. "I'd better go do my inviting before Maura's niece, Magenta, comes over to help me at the house this afternoon. I don't have phone numbers for Harriet, Maxine, or Pearl, so I'll have to talk to them in person."

Maggie called Ruth and Liz while she finished her coffee, and both women enthusiastically agreed to come to the luncheon. Fran and Ina didn't answer when she called them, so Maggie figured she'd try again later.

After tossing her empty cup in the trash can, Maggie said goodbye to June and left the shop, headed in the direction of A Fine Vintage. By the time she got to Harriet's store, the *Open* sign was out front along with the usual rack of *Irresistibles*. Maggie was tempted to browse, but she knew she didn't really have the time to spare. Instead, she entered the shop.

Inside, Harriet was arranging a display of vintage necklaces and other jewelry on a green chipped-paint dresser. She wore a sleeveless tea-length dress with red and white flowers on a soft blue background. Maggie admired her simple pearl earrings and matching white flats. *Practical for on-your-feet-all-day retail work.* While the shop wasn't as busy as opening day, a few women were browsing and Harriet's assistant, Shelby, was helping a customer at the counter.

Harriet glanced up from her arranging. "Hello, Maggie. Looking for your phone again?"

Maggie smiled. "No, Harriet. I just wanted to invite you to lunch at my home tomorrow. I thought it would be nice for some of you newer Somerset Harbor residents to meet each other and a few others in town."

Harriet seemed lost for words for a moment, then her demeanor visibly softened. "I'd love to come. Thank you. Shelby can cover for me here at the shop."

"My house is right next to Carriage House Antiques. You can't miss it."

After a few more polite words, Maggie said goodbye and set off for the library, where she found Maura, Pearl, and Magenta at the counter. All three were dressed in black today, Pearl in yet another graphic T-shirt. Maggie was beginning to enjoy seeing Pearl's shirts every time she encountered the woman. This one read, *Reader, I married him.* Maggie wondered which novel carried that line.

Maura and Pearl didn't look up from the computer screen, but Magenta, who was processing books back in, seemed eager to see her. The girl looked a little different. After a moment, Maggie realized that she wasn't wearing eyeliner today. Her face seemed brighter and softer without it.

"Hi, Mrs. Watson," Magenta said, looking genuinely pleased to see her.

"You can call me Maggie."

Magenta kept busily processing books. "Did you come to check on me about this afternoon? Don't worry, I'm coming. I didn't forget."

"I'm actually here to talk to all of you." Maggie raised her voice a little to get Maura and Pearl's attention. "I'm having a luncheon tomorrow at my house to introduce people to each other. I'd love it if you all could come."

"What a lovely idea," Maura said. "I'll be there, and Magenta can come with me." She turned toward the girl. "That is, if you want to."

Magenta had a quizzical look on her face. "Who'll be there? Anyone I know?"

Maggie grinned. Magenta was a typical youth. Maggie told her who was on her invitation list.

"No one my age, then?" Magenta glanced at Maura and seemed to reconsider. "Sounds cool, thanks."

While Maggie had been chatting with Maura and Magenta, Pearl had broken her typical habit of staring at the screen and was staring at Maggie instead.

Noticing Pearl's attention, Maggie said, "Pearl, I hope you'll come with Maura and Magenta. I would like to get to know you better, and since you're new to Somerset Harbor, I thought you might like to be introduced to some other ladies from town too."

"Please do, Pearl," Maura said. "Maggie has a lovely home. I know I'll be there with bells on."

"Why would you wear bells to a luncheon?" Pearl's question hung in the air for a moment, then she seemed to shift mental gears. "I don't usually get invitations to things." She looked at

Maggie, seemingly trying to understand an underlying motive.

Maggie smiled. "It's just a handful of us getting together, Pearl. You have to eat lunch, right? And it's a short drive to my house."

A bit of light shone in Pearl's eyes. "Yes, I have to eat lunch, and it is a short drive. I will come. Thank you."

"Wonderful," Maggie said. "I look forward to seeing you all tomorrow, and you in a few hours, Magenta." With a quick goodbye, Maggie left the library with one more stop on her agenda—Maxine's home.

However, just as she headed down the steps of the library, Maxine sped by on her patroller, again carrying a large plastic bag. And flowy white fabric was trailing out of it.

15

Maggie waved at Maxine to flag her down, but Maxine only acknowledged her with a nod and turned up Harbor Street, presumably on her way home. Maggie was beginning to realize that this was just typical Maxine behavior. Deciding not to take offense, she continued on her original course to Maxine's house. She arrived on her doorstep a few minutes later and rang the bell.

Maxine opened the door, dressed in a starched navy shirt and pants, looking much like a police officer without the insignia. "Don't tell me you're ready for another ride." She stood as straight as a gun barrel.

"Not today." Maggie smiled brightly. "I'm hoping you'll come to a lunch I'm having tomorrow. It's a mix of a few people who are new to town and a few others who've lived here longer."

Maxine stiffened even more, if that was at all possible. "I don't usually eat lunch. I just keep going until the day is done. And the weather is supposed to be good tomorrow, so it could be a big day around here with tourists and such for the patroller rentals. You said it's at your house?"

"Yes, at noon," Maggie said. "You know, in the long run, perhaps you could develop some business connections. And if you rent by the hour, maybe you could just slip over there between customers. What do you think?"

"It might work out to be a last-minute thing. Would that be all right?"

Maggie knew that was as good as it was going to get with Maxine.

"Feel free to stop by anytime you can. We'd love to have you."

Maxine bent over to tie her shoelace, giving Maggie a glimpse inside the house. Again, there were black plastic garbage bags near the entry, but this time they were untied at the top. Maggie finally saw what was inside. *Maxine's laundry?* Piles of dark clothing and white sheets overflowed from both bags, leading Maggie to assume she had interrupted Maxine just before she started folding.

Maxine stood and started closing her front door. "If you'll excuse me, I have an appointment at 1100 hours. I'll see you tomorrow. Maybe." And with that, the door shut in Maggie's face.

Back on the sidewalk, Maggie pulled her mobile phone from her pocket and tried Ina's number. Again getting no answer, Maggie figured the active septuagenarian was out hunting up gossip for her next social column. Since Fran also hadn't answered her call earlier, she thought she'd stop by The Quilt Cupboard on the way home.

As it turned out, Ina found her. Just as she was entering Fran's quilt shop, Maggie heard Ina call her name. When she turned, she saw Ina hurrying toward her with her white pin curls bouncing. "Maggie, just the woman I wanted to see."

"You look like you're on a mission." Maggie paused with her hand on the shop door. "And I was hoping to find you too. Would you like to come to Sedgwick Manor for lunch tomorrow? Just a few new friends and a few old friends."

"Who are you calling old?" There was a teasing twinkle in Ina's eye. "I'd be delighted."

"You're the last person in town I'd call old, Ina. What was it you needed?"

"Thaddeus wants a follow-up story to my big scoop on the stolen wedding dress." Ina got her notepad and pencil out of her fanny pack. "What's this I hear about a mysterious note delivered to your house?"

"What did you hear about it? You must have awfully good sources, Ina, because only a few people know about that note."

"Ah, so there is a note?"

"Did you really just trick me into verifying a rumor?" Maggie shook her head.

"Don't feel bad, sweetheart. Happens to the best of them. So how about it? What's the scoop?"

"Ina, I don't think your nephew would want me to reveal particular details about the case right now."

Ina's face fell a little. "How about suspects? What's your hunch, Maggie?" She remained poised and ready with her pencil. "Come on, you have to give me something."

"Nice try, Ina," Maggie said. "If you need a quote from me, here it is: I'm very disappointed about the loss of this possibly historic wedding dress, especially because it may have been something special relating to one of my family members. I hope it will be returned soon."

Ina was only jotting down about every third word, so Maggie didn't expect the quote in the paper to be much like the one she had just given.

"I guess that'll do. Are you headed in here?" Ina indicated the quilt shop.

"I'm here to invite Fran to lunch too." Maggie opened the door. "Are you coming in?"

"Yeah, I need something."

Maggie held the door open for Ina, and they approached Fran at the front counter.

"Hi, you two," Fran said. "What's up?"

Ina went first. "You have any red thread?"

"Of course," Fran said, pointing to a retail display next to the counter. "Cherry, scarlet, or fire-engine?"

Ina thought for a moment. "I'll take all three."

"What are you making?" Fran asked, tilting her head sideways as Ina placed the three different spools on the counter.

"Nobody likes a busybody, dear," Ina said, handing over cash for the thread. "Now Maggie, are you sure you don't have any more information you might want to include in the article? I certainly wouldn't want my facts to go astray of the truth."

Maggie choked back a laugh at Ina's double standard. "No, Ina."

"Worth a shot. Better get my notes over to Thaddeus so he can update my blug. Thanks for the thread, Fran. See you both later."

Watching Ina exit the shop, Maggie wondered what the tech-savvy Pearl would make of Ina. *Well, there's an icebreaker for tomorrow. Maybe she can share some of her Internet knowledge with Ina at lunch.* She was glad that Ina would be coming to her luncheon, although she hoped her curious and incorrigible friend would leave her notepad and pencil at home.

Fran shook her head as Ina departed, her pert ponytail swaying gently. "Do you need three shades of red thread too, Maggie?"

"Not today. I'm wondering if you're free at noon tomorrow. I'm having a luncheon at my house."

Fran shook her head again. "Sorry, I'm doing an advanced binding workshop tomorrow afternoon and I have to get set up. Have fun, though."

"I'm sure we will. I hope you have a good turnout."

"I hope you do too," Fran said. "Who all is coming?"

"Ruth, Ina, Daisy, Liz, and June, of course. And I also invited Maura O'Brien and her niece, as well as some other new faces in town: Harriet Hamstead, Maxine MacDonald, and the new library volunteer, Pearl Winters."

"I know Pearl. She was just in here yesterday with an antique lace coverlet she needed advice on repairing. She said she just bought a new bed at your shop and she wants to fix the coverlet before the furniture is delivered."

She must have been carrying her coverlet out of the alley yesterday. Maggie gently chastised herself for ever thinking quiet Pearl was wandering around town with the stolen flapper gown in a dress bag. "An antique coverlet will be perfect for the bed she purchased."

"She doesn't seem like the type to decorate her home in Victorian style, considering her wardrobe of black T-shirts," Fran said, then smiled. "But I do love it when people are full of pleasant surprises."

"It does keep life interesting." Maggie checked the time. "I'd better get going. Good luck with your class tomorrow."

"Thanks. Enjoy your luncheon. I look forward to hearing all about it."

After exchanging farewells with Fran, Maggie left the shop. As she turned toward home, she saw Harriet barreling down the road at the wheel of Beulah the '57 Chevy Bel Air. Harriet waved as she passed, then disappeared around a corner with a faint squeal of tires. *Perhaps it was Harriet herself who was the reckless driver a few mornings ago, rather than Maxine.* Maggie made a mental note to steer clear of Harriet and Beulah when she was on the road.

In a matter of minutes, Maggie was heading up the walkway to Sedgwick Manor, only to find Magenta sitting on the front steps. The girl was looking down at her phone, pink-tipped hair in her face, but she rose when she caught sight of Maggie.

Maggie glanced at her watch. Somehow a whole morning had vanished as she made her rounds about town. She had thought she'd have enough time to grab a bit of lunch before Magenta got there, but perhaps the girl would like something with her.

"Magenta, you're early."

"Is that okay? Sorry, I finished at the library and didn't have anywhere else to be."

"It's fine. I'm just sorry you were sitting here by yourself. Would you like some lunch before we get started?"

"Yes, please," Magenta said as she followed Maggie into the house. In the kitchen, Maggie expected the girl to plop down at a counter stool and watch. But instead, she insisted on helping Maggie make turkey sandwiches and a couple of simple salads with vinaigrette. They moved to the breakfast room table, where Maggie asked Magenta about herself as they ate.

As it turned out, Magenta had an older brother. "He's good at everything, Maggie. Everything. He's on his college crew team. At Yale. And he's in student government. And he's volunteering in Africa this summer. How do I compete with that?"

"You don't have to, Magenta," Maggie said after taking a sip of her iced tea. "You are yourself. I'm sure your parents only expect you to do your best. School is just a transitory thing. It's temporary, something you have to go through to reach the goals you have for yourself. Just find what you love to do and make that your life's work."

"I like to read," Magenta said. "That's about all. Well, and I like to make things right, put them in order, like at the library."

"Yes, I've seen that quality in you. If you feel most comfortable in a library, why not be a librarian? Or a fiction buyer for a bookstore? Or a book editor? There are lots of options out there. I've heard that more books are being published now than ever. Someone like you, with a good eye for literature, could be a real asset in the right setting."

"Yeah, maybe." Magenta spoke shyly, but Maggie sensed that she was processing her advice.

"Speaking of libraries, shall we get started in mine?"

"Sure. I'll do the dishes first, though." Magenta picked up her own empty glass and plate as well as Maggie's and took them to the kitchen sink, where she washed and dried them.

Maggie watched her wipe the counter and dry off the sink. *Now there's a good kid. She just needs a little stability.*

A few minutes later, they entered the library. Magenta walked around the room, apparently assessing the shelves of books and probably wondering where to start. "I'll at least separate the fiction from the nonfiction books for starters," she said at last. "Then you can decide how detailed you want to get with each category."

"That sounds great," Maggie said. "Would you like some paper and a pencil?"

"Sure." Magenta climbed the rolling ladder and examined the top shelf. "Hey, look at this." She pulled out a leather-bound book and turned toward Maggie.

"What is it?" Maggie's voice trembled. Magenta's casual stance on the ladder made her a little nervous.

"It's a copy of *Jane Eyre*. Guess you didn't need to borrow one from the public library after all." Magenta positioned herself on the ladder so she was facing into the room, her feet on the third rung from the bottom. She leaned back against the ladder and opened the book's front cover and gazed at the page.

"Magenta, I don't mean to be a nag, but you're making me nervous. Could you hold on to something, please?"

Magenta grinned at Maggie, then nodded. She closed the book, turned around on the ladder, and replaced the book on the shelf.

Maggie retrieved a legal pad and a pencil from the office, then returned to the library and handed them to Magenta. "I'll just let you work in here for a while. If you need anything, I'll be in the office."

"Sure, cool," Magenta said distractedly.

Maggie paid bills and answered e-mails in the office while Magenta toiled away in the library. Every so often, Maggie would hear the thump of a stack of books being placed on the ground or the creak of the ladder's wheels as it was pushed along its track.

At the end of the afternoon, the library was in an orderly disarray, with neat piles of books stacked around the perimeter. Magenta needed to get home for dinner, but she promised to pick right up where she had left off next time.

When Maggie walked Magenta out, the girl thanked Maggie for giving her the job. "And thanks for the pep talk earlier." Magenta pushed her hair off her face. "I feel better—like there's some hope for me."

"There's always hope, Magenta," Maggie said. "And I could use you tomorrow morning too. Can you come over early to help me prepare the food and set the table?"

"Sure," Magenta said. "I'll be here. Bye." With that, she bounded down the front steps and down the sidewalk to the street.

Maggie returned to the office to turn off her computer. As she did, her eyes settled on a framed picture of her mother with Aunt Evelyn and Aunt Sharon. She checked her watch. She had just enough time to give Aunt Sharon a call before the Dancing With the Seniors contest. She originally hadn't thought that her aunt would be able to shed light on the dress's history, but now that the gown was missing, Maggie felt as though she ought to try anything to learn more about it.

Sharon lived in the southern part of Maine and was the youngest and only one of the three McCrary sisters still living. Maggie loved Sharon for her energy and enthusiasm. She was always the life of the party.

"Maggie, dear, to what do I owe the pleasure?" Sharon's familiar voice was music to Maggie's ears.

"It's a long story. Earlier this week, I found a wedding dress in one of the closets upstairs, and I'm wondering if you know anything about it."

"What sort of wedding dress?"

"It seems to be from sometime in the 1920s, designed by Jean Patierre."

"Wow, Jean Patierre? You know I couldn't care less about antiques, but even I've heard of him."

"Did you know that he attended a Fourth of July party here at Sedgwick Manor in 1928?" Maggie asked. "Apparently your grandparents threw some memorable parties back then."

"I had no idea, actually. That dress must be worth gobs of money."

"I'm more concerned about its value as a family heirloom." Maggie walked into the master suite and ran her fingers across the top of the polished wood jewelry box that held the rings. "I don't think the dress was ever worn. And there were two rings in the pocket and a veil that was torn from bottom to top."

"Sounds scandalous."

"Could be. Did you ever hear anything about a romance gone wrong or a wedding planned for Sedgwick Manor that never took place?"

"Maggie, dear, you know family genealogy and history are not my forte. I do remember hearing something about an older relative. It was someone related to my grandfather, your great-grandfather."

"Franklin?" Maggie asked. "He's the one who hosted the parties."

"Yes. But I'm afraid I don't know any of the details. My best guess would be that the dress does come from family. Otherwise, I imagine Evelyn would have sold it in the antiques store."

"Thanks, Aunt Sharon."

"Sorry I can't give you any more information," Sharon said. "Now tell me, how's that sweet girl of yours?"

Maggie gave Sharon an update on Emily, then wished her a good night with a promise to visit later in the summer. Having been wandering around the room while they chatted, Maggie found that she'd ended up in front of her closet door, where the veil still hung. She'd have to figure out what to do with that eventually. Maybe it was even repairable. She made a mental note to ask Fran about it the next time she saw her. *Now, what to wear to the Dancing With the Seniors contest?*

She hoped she wouldn't be dragged out onto the dance floor but decided she should be prepared for anything. The swishy skirt and soft yellow cardigan-and-shell set she had purchased yesterday at A Fine Vintage would be perfect. She changed, freshened her hair and makeup, then headed out the door.

On the drive to the VFW hall, Maggie rolled down the windows of her white Volkswagen Jetta and let the fresh June evening air swirl around her. She felt more relaxed on the short drive than she had all week. She was almost disappointed to find herself parking in front of the VFW building, a low brick structure with white pillars flanking the entrance. A light breeze had set the series of armed forces and American flags out front waving gently.

After trotting up the steps, Maggie entered the open double doors to find an older man in his service hat stationed at a receiving table. Maggie paid her five-dollar entry fee, which included tea or coffee and as many cookies as she liked from the refreshments table, then entered the auditorium.

A large stage was opposite the entry doors, and chairs lined the other three walls. A disk jockey stationed in a corner was playing lively jazz music. Pairs of dance contestants with numbers pinned to their clothing were warming up around the edges of the room. Maggie admired the ladies dressed in elegant 1920s-inspired dresses and headbands that went across their foreheads. Some were clearly homemade costumes put together with items close at hand, but Maggie still felt transported back in time. A little less splashy but still quite dapper, the gentlemen wore slacks, shirts, suspenders, and bow ties for the most part.

Looking around, Maggie spotted June and her parents near the stage. They saw her as well and waved. As she walked toward June, Maggie recognized several other couples, mostly from church. As one practicing pair shimmied off to the side, another all-too-familiar face was revealed—Ina.

Standing near a tall, slender gentleman wearing black slacks, a white long-sleeved shirt, black suspenders, and a red bow tie, Ina wore a bright red flapper dress with layers of long fringe, and she had a red ribbon with an artificial red dahlia around her forehead. She also wore a nervous expression, but it turned to delight when she spotted Maggie approaching.

"Maggie!" Ina said, then clip-clopped toward her in strappy silver sandals, undoubtedly the ones she'd found at A Fine Vintage.

"Ina, you look sensational. Why didn't you tell any of us you were dancing tonight?"

"To tell you the truth, I didn't know if I'd make it. Frankly I'm just doing this as a favor for old Ernest over there." She aimed her thumb toward her partner. "He used to be a professional dancer, you know. Really top-notch. I'm no match for him."

"Nonsense, Ina. I'm sure you'll be perfect."

"I wouldn't be so sure. He's got a good twelve inches on me." Ina rolled her eyes. "His real partner came down with the flu this week so he asked me to fill in. I figured it might be fun, and it'll certainly be healthy."

"You're a champ." Maggie shifted her focus to Ernest as he strode gracefully over. "Wonderful to meet you, Ernest. I'm Ina's friend, Maggie. It'll be a treat to see you two dance this evening."

"Indeed." Maggie sensed uncertainty in the man's deep voice. "Ina, I think we ought to go over the pivot turns again."

"You're the boss, Ernie. Let's go."

Maggie watched as the pair warmed up. Partially leaned forward, they'd step back and forth. They held their arms at an angle in front of their bodies with fingers pointed up, alternately raising and lowering opposite elbows. It looked chaotic, and not in the controlled way she saw in the other couples. Every minute or so, Ernest would stop and whisper something to Ina, who would look at her feet in concentration and then nod and try again.

Maggie thought they were really starting to get in a groove when Ina suddenly cried out and fell to the floor.

16

Maggie rushed over, and she and Ernest helped Ina hop to a chair.

"It's my right knee," Ina said, holding it. "I think I twisted something." She stood and tried to put weight on her leg, but then she yelped in pain and sat down.

Maggie remembered the time Emily had torn the cartilage in one of her knees skiing, and she was afraid that had happened to Ina. Ernest brought over a chair and set it in front of Ina, then helped her position her leg on it.

June had run over when she saw what happened. "Don't move, Ina," she said. "I'll go get you some ice from the cooler."

Ernest sighed. "I suppose we will have to withdraw from the contest. Pity."

Ina looked at him and then at Maggie. "Maggie, you could take my place."

"Oh, no no," Maggie said. She glanced at Ernest and saw a horrified expression flash through his eyes that matched her own sentiments. "I have no idea which foot to put where."

"I do," said a voice behind her.

Maggie whirled to see Harriet, dressed to the nines in the most spectacular flapper dress Maggie had ever seen. Besides her missing wedding dress, of course.

"Harriet, what are you saying?" Maggie asked. "You can dance?"

"You bet I can," Harriet said with no small amount of pride. "Two-times Charleston dance champ at the YWCA in Boston." She demonstrated with full enthusiasm.

Ina looked at Ernest. "Could you make a last-minute substitution?

I don't see how it could be any worse than not competing. Or trying to compete with me, healthy or not."

"What have we got to lose?" Ernest stood a little straighter. "I'll go let our judges know." He dodged gracefully through the practicing couples across the floor toward the registration table.

Ina beamed at Harriet. "Thank you, dear. Truth be told, I don't think I would have lasted a minute with these silly sandals on. I prefer my walking shoes, you know."

When Ernest returned, he took Harriet around the floor for a few minutes of warm-up. Maggie smiled and thought they were quite the couple, swinging their legs and arms in rhythm to the music. It didn't hurt, she supposed, that Harriet was a little closer to Ernest in stature than little Ina.

A hush fell over the crowd as a woman dressed in a gold flapper dress walked to the middle of the stage with a handheld microphone and welcomed everyone to the competition. She introduced three judges, who sat at a table on the stage next to the DJ. A few moments later, the first couple took to the floor and danced up a storm.

Ina, now with a bag of ice draped over her knee courtesy of June, provided commentary to Maggie, explaining the various steps: knee slaps, scissor kicks, crazy legs, the helicopter, the flying Charleston, the around-the-world Charleston, and more. Just the names of the moves made Maggie dizzy. She could hardly imagine doing them.

As the dancers progressed, Ernest kept asking Harriet, "Can you do that?" and Harriet repeatedly said yes.

Maggie loved the jazzy music with all the brass instruments and tapped her feet as she watched.

Finally, it was Ernest and Harriet's turn. With a jig kick they were off, covering the whole dance floor with the audience cheering them on. Maggie was amazed. For a couple just thrown together with no time to master any kind of routine, Ernest and

Harried looked like professionals who had practiced for this particular event for months. After they had exhausted their shared repertoire, which was huge and included a series of aerial moves, the couple finished with a face-to-face pose in the middle of the floor. The crowd went wild.

Ernest and Harriet bowed and came back to their chairs by Ina and Maggie, grabbing water bottles and catching their breath while they all waited for the results.

Ina said, "Ernest, I believe you have found the perfect dance partner. Thank you, Harriet."

It wasn't so dark in the auditorium that Maggie couldn't see Harriet blush as she nodded in acknowledgement.

"So Harriet, what brought you here tonight?" Maggie asked, making conversation while the judges deliberated.

Harriet gave Maggie a pinched smile. "Let's just say someone helped me realize that I need to open myself up a little more to new experiences, to put myself out there and make friends."

"Never a bad idea," Maggie said, pleased that her advice had been received so well. "We're glad you're here. You saved Ernest tonight."

"I overheard some customers looking for flapper dresses for the competition earlier, and I figured I'd come by. Besides, I couldn't leave this hot little number stuck in the back of my closet." Harriet ran her fingers through some of the fringe, and the beads on her dress sparkled.

"It is as showstopping as your dancing. Where did you get it?"

"Come now, a girl needs her secrets. I didn't steal it out of a shop window, that's for certain."

Taken aback at the return of Harriet's razor tongue, Maggie said nothing. Her silence went unnoticed as the woman in the gold dress returned to the stage with her microphone.

"Thank you all again for coming out tonight," she said. "It is with great pleasure that I announce the first-place winners of the Dancing With the Seniors Charleston dancing competition: Ernest Streeter and Harriet Hamstead!"

Reassured that Ernest would see Ina safely home, Maggie congratulated the couple, said her goodbyes, and left the auditorium with the departing crowd. She waved to June and her parents, who had come in a respectable third in the competition.

A short while later, Maggie had parked the Jetta and was starting up the walkway to Sedgwick Manor, an extra bounce in her step after watching all those folks almost twice her age do the Charleston. But as she looked toward her home, she felt a prickly sensation in her spine. Something was wrong.

She distinctly remembered leaving several lights on, but the house was pitch-black. Clouds that had blown in after sunset covered the moon, casting dark shadows everywhere she looked, so she stepped carefully the rest of the way to the front door. Crickets chirped around the edges of the lawn, and a cool, soft wind coming from the harbor whispered through the trees. She thought she heard toads croaking in the distance.

Everything seemed alive in the darkness that surrounded her.

Maggie found her way up the walkway and, to get her bearings, felt for one of the two brick posts at the bottom of the half dozen steps that led to the house. Then she froze. A pattering sound of some kind. *Snickers? Not unless he is now wearing shoes.* Maggie let out a huff of nervous laughter despite herself. She was beginning to imagine things.

The sound was getting closer and closer. Maggie paused at the door, listening. As she put her hand on the knob, she felt it turning from the other side.

The knob was yanked from her hand as the door flew open. There was a flash of white as a figure rushed at her, and that was the last thing she remembered.

17

The waves were lapping over her, but Maggie couldn't move. How would she get back to shore? The dark sea had enveloped her, and she was helpless against its pull. Maggie tried and failed to open her eyes. A sudden speck of light was growing in the distance—so close, yet so far. She struggled to get above the increasingly larger waves but she couldn't move fast enough. Darkness was enclosing her.

Maggie opened her eyes. Snickers, with paws on her chest, was meowing at her. He had been sniffing her face and worriedly licking her nose with his rough tongue. She wasn't in the sea. She was lying on her back across the threshold of the open front door.

Her head throbbed. She slowly pushed herself up to a sitting position. Her surroundings spun. Snickers crawled into her lap, and Maggie sat still and concentrated on his purring and his warmth until her eyes focused and she got her bearings. What was she doing in her open doorway in the middle of the night? Her memory returned: Someone had been in Sedgwick Manor and knocked her over as he or she exited.

Maggie felt the back of her head. Yes, there was a lump where she had hit the floor. Should she call 911? Other than the bump, she was physically fine.

She stood and felt for the light switch, but when she flipped it, nothing happened. *And now the power is out? Just great.*

Maggie retrieved her purse from the doorway where it had fallen. Fortunately it looked as if nothing had been taken from it, and she pulled out her phone. She turned on the built-in flashlight, then used it to find her way out the front door and along the bushes toward the back of the house. She fought off a rising sense of dread in the darkness as she stumbled toward the breaker box. She was thankful Snickers was following her. *If there were only more light.* Maggie looked toward Shoreline Drive. The streetlights were on, so there wasn't a general power failure.

She looked up again at the clouds firmly blocking out the moonlight, then continued on her mission.

Finally, she located the metal breaker box, opened it, and flipped the switches off, then on. The lights in the house illuminated immediately. Slightly relieved but still on edge, Maggie went back around to the front door, where she hesitated before entering. She locked the door behind her with a firm *click.*

In the kitchen, she made an ice pack to hold on the back of her head while she looked through the rest of the house. She methodically walked through the first floor, looking around at the furnishings and collectibles. Living areas, foyer, library, office—nothing seemed disturbed. Until she walked from her bathroom into her walk-in closet. A hanger was on the floor. She looked up at the closet door and went cold.

The veil was gone.

First the dress, now the veil. Someone wanted the whole wedding ensemble. Maggie checked the wooden box on her dresser for the wedding rings she had found in the dress pocket. She sighed in relief. They were there.

Now for the upstairs. Holding on to the staircase railing, she took the steps slowly, aware of her lightheadedness. After a sweep of all the bedrooms and closets, she was fairly certain that nothing else was missing or out of place.

A wave of dizziness hit, and Maggie swayed. *I should lie down.* Maggie carefully made her way back downstairs to her bedroom and lay down on her bed, letting her pillow cradle the ice pack in place. She pulled out her cell phone and started to dial the police department but had second thoughts as a heavy blanket of weariness enveloped her. An investigation could wait until the morning. All she wanted to do was sleep.

. . . .

The next morning dawned bright and clear, the clouds from the previous evening having blown away in the night. Fortunately, Maggie's headache had dissipated like the clouds, and all that remained was a little tenderness at the lump on the back of her head. After getting ready for the day, she called Officer Linton, who insisted on coming over right away.

When Maggie heard his police cruiser pull up, she greeted him at the front door. "We have to stop meeting like this."

"It's no time for jokes, Maggie," Robert said. "You should have called last night and someone would have come over to secure your home. Not to mention checked out the bump on your head."

Maggie sighed, then led Robert into the house. "I don't think I could have kept my eyes open that long. Anyway, no real harm done. I'm fine."

"*Fine* is not the word I'd use," Robert said severely. "Now why don't you take me through what happened when you got home last night?"

Maggie thought for a moment. "The house was dark. I heard a pattering sound, maybe feet coming down the staircase. I started turning the door handle, but someone was turning it from the inside. That scared me, of course. And then there was this flash of white against the darkness. And then I don't remember any more."

"Could the flash of white, as you call it, have been the veil you said was stolen?" he asked.

"Yes, it could," she said, "especially since I found it missing a short time later."

Just then there was a knock at the door. Maggie looked at her watch. It was barely eight. She opened the door to find

Magenta, dressed in black skinny jeans, a dark pink tie-dyed tank top, and a smile.

"Am I interrupting something?" she asked, glancing at Officer Linton. "I can come back later."

Maggie thought the girl looked nervous but quickly dismissed the idea. Many youngsters tended to feel uncomfortable around police officers. "No, Magenta, I think we're wrapping up." She looked to Robert to confirm.

"Yes, all done here," he said, slipping his notepad into his shirt pocket. "I'll get back with you, Maggie, if something comes up." He looked her straight in the eye. "And give me a call if you need anything at all."

Maggie thanked him and saw him out.

"Is everything all right, Maggie?" Magenta's nervousness had been replaced by concern.

There was no point in alarming the girl. "Just a little issue here last night. Nothing for you to worry about. Now let's get prepping."

In the kitchen, Magenta chopped a variety of summer fruits while Maggie made chicken salad and egg salad. She would set the salads out with sliced croissants and garnishes so everyone could make their own sandwiches at lunch.

Magenta finished cutting a cantaloupe into chunks. She reached for a carton of washed strawberries to start slicing them but hesitated. "Maggie, why were the police here?"

Maggie took a deep breath. Should she mention the break-in, the burglary, her knockout? She decided to keep things simple. "I came home last night to find someone in my house. I didn't really see who it was—the house lights were off. As I opened the front door, someone rushed out and knocked me over. Then when I checked the house, I found that something I value had been stolen."

"You got knocked over?" Magenta said. "Were you okay?"

"I was knocked unconscious when my head hit the floor."

Maggie washed an heirloom tomato and cut it into slices to serve with the sandwiches.

"Knocked out?" Magenta said. "I didn't know . . . I mean, you seem okay now though."

Maggie smiled slightly. "Yes, I'm fine. My head is sore, but I'm fine otherwise."

"Wow, that's scary," Magenta said. "I'm sorry that happened to you, and I hope you get your stuff back. Whatever it was."

As the two continued prepping, Maggie told Magenta a little about each woman she had invited to the luncheon—how they met and what each person did. During a lull in the conversation, Maggie found herself watching Magenta as the girl arranged fruit artistically on two large white ironstone platters. Could it have been Magenta who had been in her home last night? She shook off the thought and contemplated another. *Why would someone steal a ripped wedding veil? It just doesn't make sense.* She hoped Officer Linton would have some answers for her, but she wouldn't be surprised if he came up empty-handed.

While Magenta was cleaning up the kitchen, Maggie set the dining room table with silverware, yellow linen napkins, and Aunt Evelyn's Hammersley bone china dotted with white, purple, and yellow pansies.

"Wow, looks really fancy," Magenta said, coming up behind Maggie as she placed the last teacup and saucer on the table. "I'm done in the kitchen. Anything else?"

Maggie had just a few errands to run. "Would you like to go into town with me to get some flowers? You could help me pick out a couple bouquets." Maggie pointed at the crystal vases she had in mind for the arrangements.

"Sure, that would be cool," Magenta said. "Let me check with Aunt Maura—she might need me at the library." Magenta got out her cell phone, dialed, and stepped into the foyer. A couple of minutes later she returned to the dining room. "She said it's fine."

Maggie checked the back and side door locks, then grabbed her keys and purse. After she and Magenta went out through the front door, she inserted her key in the lock and turned it, then jiggled the knob to make sure it was locked. She wasn't taking any chances this morning.

They got in the Jetta and Maggie drove them to The Singing Mermaid, where Magenta chose a mix of roses, peonies, and lilies. Maggie thought they would be the perfect finishing touch to the table.

The next stop was The Busy Bean. Maggie and Magenta walked in and approached the register. A crowd of Somerset Harbor teenagers were grouped at the counter nearby, apparently waiting for Daisy to whip up some frozen coffees.

"Hi, Daisy," Maggie said when Daisy turned off the blender and noticed her. "New blender?"

"Gotta give the people what they want," Daisy said, filling two clear plastic cups with blended iced coffee. She squirted a generous dollop of whipped cream on top and shook on a few sprinkles from a plastic shaker. She added a lid, then set the cups and some straws on the counter in front of the teens. "Here you are, kids."

"This looks awesome, Mrs. Carter," one of the teenagers said. "Thanks!"

"You're welcome, hon. Enjoy." Daisy turned her attention to Maggie. "Here to pick up your desserts?"

"Yes, and some croissants too. And—" Maggie noticed that Magenta's gaze was following the teenagers as they walked away with their iced coffees. "Mocha or vanilla bean, Magenta?"

"I usually drink coffee black, no fussy stuff." Magenta eyed the blender, then smiled. "But why not? Mocha, I guess."

Maggie pulled out her wallet. "And two mocha frappés, as big as they come, Daisy. With extra whipped cream."

"It'll be my pleasure. You're Maura's niece, aren't you?"

Daisy asked. Magenta nodded. "I figured as much. You look like a smart one, just like her."

Magenta gave her a shy smile.

A short while later, Maggie and Magenta were back in the Sedgwick Manor kitchen, continuing to prepare for the luncheon and savoring their indulgent frozen drinks.

While Magenta snipped the flowers and placed them just so in the vases, Maggie washed out her favorite teapots. The conversation turned to Magenta's home life.

"So what does your mom do for a living?" Maggie asked.

"She's a lecturer at Amherst College. She used to be a newspaper reporter, and she still does some freelance writing."

"What kinds of English classes does she teach?"

"Argumentation." Magenta laughed. "My mom says that everything is an argument. And that pretty much describes our relationship."

"And your dad," Maggie said, "what does he do?"

"He taught at the college too, until my parents separated. Political science. Everything was an argument with them as well. He's a free thinker, likes to explore ideas. Mom likes things neatly arranged in boxes—her way." Magenta looked at Maggie. "They were incompatible."

"And how would you describe yourself?" Maggie asked. "Are you a free thinker or a box arranger?"

Magenta looked up to the ceiling contemplatively. "I do like things neat. You've probably noticed that. But I try to think creatively too, to problem solve."

"I think that's a very healthy way to be. Speaking of creative problem solving, I'm hoping that Officer Linton will find the missing dress and veil."

Magenta's attention remained focused on the flowers she was arranging. Every so often, she'd turn the vase and examine the bouquet from all angles. Occasionally she would remove a bloom and snip the stem, then tuck it back into the container. After silence had reigned for a few seconds, she looked at Maggie expectantly.

Maggie realized Magenta was waiting for her to expound. "It was a veil I lost last night."

"Hmmm," Magenta said. "Did it go with the dress?"

"Yes." Maggie explained how she had hoped that, despite having the dress stolen, the veil might still offer some clue to the mysterious wedding that never was. "Now the veil is gone too. It's like a piece of my family history has been torn away from me. I'm just hoping that whoever has the dress and the veil will do the right thing and return them."

Magenta met Maggie's eyes. "You think I took it, don't you?"

"No, I—I honestly don't know what to think." Maggie wanted to believe that no one would intentionally hurt her and steal her things, least of all Magenta. But the truth was, someone had. "I'm just hoping the things come back to me. Soon."

They fell silent again as Magenta finished arranging, then she and Maggie carried the two crystal vases to the dining room. They each set one on opposite ends of the table.

Maggie stood back and smiled.

"It looks perfect, Maggie," Magenta said, her voice flat. "You will all have a great time today."

"You're coming, right?" Maggie tipped her head.

"I don't know." Magenta avoided eye contact.

"But who will help me serve all the tea and goodies? There's still a lot to—"

"I guess you'll just have to manage without me!" Magenta threw down the towel she had used to wipe water droplets off the vases and ran to the front door.

"Magenta?"

But Magenta was already out the door, slamming it behind her.

18

There was less than an hour left before guests arrived and she had now lost Magenta's help, so Maggie had to hustle. First task—get dressed. She put on the salmon-hued sheath she had gotten at A Fine Vintage, hoping Harriet would notice and be pleased. Maggie slipped into strappy white sandals, which would be comfy for entertaining, freshened up her hair, and dabbed on some tinted lip gloss.

Worried about Magenta, she texted Maura. *Magenta left a little bit ago. She seemed upset. Not sure where she was headed.*

A few moments later, she got a reply. *She just walked in the door here. She's having a hard time right now. Thanks for giving her chances.*

Still concerned, but grateful that the girl had gone back to her aunt, Maggie went to the kitchen and put on an apron over her dress. She saw Magenta's abandoned coffee on the counter and sighed as she dumped it out and tossed the cup into the trash. She carried the fruit platters Magenta had arranged to the dining room table, then brought the rest of the food as well. Finally, she heated water for tea, poured it into the teapots, and put it out along with a selection of tea bags.

When the doorbell rang, Maggie took her apron off and headed to answer it.

Maxine MacDonald, dressed in starched navy blue today, was right on time. Maggie thought Maxine almost saluted.

"You said noon, right?" Maxine asked, left arm behind her. "Here, I brought flowers." She thrust a simple bouquet of daisies toward Maggie.

Maggie was surprised by such a sentimental gesture from straitlaced Maxine. *No matter how well you think you have someone figured out, they can still surprise you.*

"I adore daisies, thank you," Maggie said.

"I guessed. When you were at my house, you looked at my daisies a lot," Maxine said. "When you weren't trying to peek inside."

"A character in a movie once said daisies are such a friendly flower. I've always liked that. Please come in and make yourself at home."

Maxine entered the foyer. Maggie waited at the door when she saw Ruth and Daisy coming up the walk. They were followed by Ina, who was limping and leaning on Liz's arm for support. Just then, June appeared from around the side of the house, having walked over from Carriage House Antiques.

Maggie welcomed them all inside and reintroduced them to Maxine.

"Who could forget meeting this lady? I loved buzzing around on that contraption of hers," Ina said. "Not that I'll be doing much patrolling anytime soon. Doctor said it's a bad twist. I told him we were doing the Charleston, not the twist, but he wasn't amused."

"I'm glad it's not more serious, Ina. Why don't you go into the dining room and get settled?" Maggie gestured toward the dining room, and her guests followed her suggestion.

She turned back to the front door when she heard the screech of tires outside. Pearl stood in the doorway wearing a black T-shirt with white printing that read, *Beware, for I am fearless and therefore powerful. —Mary Shelley.*

Behind Pearl, Maggie could see Beulah the Bel Air on the street and Harriet walking up in coral high heels, matching earrings, and a gray dress with a full skirt and sheer overlay. "Hello, Maggie," Harriet said. "Sorry, but I can only stay for about an hour, I'm afraid."

"I'm so glad you could come at all. Both of you. Please come in." Maggie guided Harriet and Pearl, who hadn't yet said a word, into the dining room. The other ladies turned their attention to Maggie when she entered the room, so she welcomed them all again. "Most of you know each other, but I'd like to introduce Pearl Winters. She is volunteering at the library with Maura, who I hope will be here soon."

"You're working at the library?" Liz asked Pearl. "How wonderful. Are you a real bookworm?"

"I'm human, not a worm," Pearl said, to Liz's clear astonishment. "But I do prefer reading to any other recreational activity."

"We have a reading group at Old Faith Chapel if you're interested," Liz said, recovering quickly. "I'd be happy to get you in touch with the lady who runs it."

Maggie smiled at Liz's welcoming nature and was reassured that her attempt to help the new town residents forge friendships had potential for success. She greeted everyone individually, then encouraged them to sit down with Ina at the table. Once everyone was seated, they took turns selecting their food and tea, chatting politely all the while.

The doorbell rang, and Maggie excused herself to answer it. When she opened the door, she found Maura, her face a bit flushed. Somewhat surprisingly, Magenta stood behind her. "Sorry we're late, Maggie," Maura said. "We had a few . . . issues to discuss." She raised an eyebrow and glanced sideways at her niece, whose own gaze was steadily focused on the ground.

Maggie said that was fine and ushered them to seats in the dining room. "I think most of you know Maura. Staying with her this summer is her niece, Mary Catherine. She prefers to be called Magenta."

Maura politely waved, but Magenta barely looked up as she received the serving plates of food.

Maggie turned to Maxine. "So, Maxine, how did you decide to move to Somerset Harbor?"

Maxine chewed her bite of food and swallowed. "I was in the army with this guy who spent summers here growing up," she said. "He made it sound like a nice-enough place, and I didn't have anywhere else I wanted to be after I got tired of Boston."

"We're glad you chose it." Maggie addressed Pearl. "What about you, Pearl? What brought you here?"

Pearl's eyes remained on her plate. "I ran out of gas," she said quietly.

"I'm sorry, what was that?" Maggie asked.

"I ran out of gas," Pearl repeated, a little louder. "I was driving up the coast, and I ran out of gas here. The man at the gas station was very polite. I decided it was as good a place as any to retire."

"My reason is a little better," Harriet said, giving pointed looks to both Maxine and Pearl. "*I* followed my heart." She laid a hand on her chest.

"Ooh, tell us more," Daisy said, leaning in.

"Not in the way you think," Harriet said. "As you know, I have a thing for classic dresses. My favorite designer of all time is the incomparable Jean Patierre." She said his name with a practiced French accent, then paused for effect. Seeing that her audience was suitably entranced, she continued. "It turns out that Monsieur Patierre moved to New York City after World War I, and he spent his summers here in Somerset Harbor. I figured that if I was going to open a business selling vintage clothing, I should do it somewhere that was deemed worthy by an artistic genius."

"Jean Patierre designed my wedding dress," Maggie said. "I mean, the flapper dress that was stolen."

"Then it was truly priceless," Harriet said. "He only designed one wedding dress in his entire career, and that must have been it.

He was very private, so I don't know many details. The story goes that he met a young couple at the same party where they got engaged, here in Somerset Harbor. He was so taken with their love story that he wanted to commemorate it by designing her wedding dress."

"Just goes to show you never know who you'll meet at a party in Somerset Harbor," Daisy said, and everyone laughed.

Conversation was easy after that as the luncheon flowed from sandwiches to dessert. Everyone raved over Daisy's chocolate mousse cups, and Maggie thought Pearl looked the happiest she had ever seen her when the stoic librarian took her first bite.

Soon the lunch hour was up. At one o'clock, most of the ladies said they needed to be leaving. Maggie was pleased when Magenta stood and began clearing plates from the table, and she smiled when Maura joined her.

"Thank you all so much for coming," Maggie said as she and most of her guests got up. Ruth and the injured Ina, who said they had nowhere to be, remained at the table discussing the previous evening's dance contest. June excused herself, saying she would head back to the antiques shop through the side door.

The mealtime conversation continued as the rest of the crowd moved through the foyer, out the front door, and down the walkway to the street. Daisy and Liz headed toward downtown on the sidewalk. Harriet climbed into Beulah the Bel Air, Maxine stepped onto her transporter, and Pearl got into a vintage Volkswagen Beetle.

Maggie watched and waved goodbye to them all but realized too late how poor her timing was. Harriet, Maxine, and Pearl all waved back and, apparently distracted by their farewells, didn't realize that they were all reversing toward one another.

And in what seemed like slow motion, Maggie realized that Officer Linton was driving up to the house while all three women's vehicles were converging in reverse.

"Look out!" Maggie yelled, pointing.

Too late. All four vehicles had connected with a series of excruciatingly loud metal-on-metal sound effects.

Maggie rushed to the crash site and took stock of who might need help first. Officer Linton jumped out of his squad car to check the others.

Maxine, who fortunately was helmeted, was sitting on the ground, a bit dazed, but otherwise all right. Nothing bleeding that Maggie could see. Her patroller lay on the ground, but Maxine had jumped at the last second and didn't take any of the impact herself.

Harriet was slowly getting out of her Bel Air. She was just as steady on her high heels as she had been at the luncheon—but there was a good-sized scratch in the paint on the rear fender. "Beulah!" she wailed.

Pearl was frozen at the wheel of her Beetle, still seat-belted, staring ahead. Maggie leaned through the passenger-side window, which was rolled down. "Pearl, are you all right?"

Pearl looked down and around at herself, hands still gripping the steering wheel. "I don't know. I thought I was dead for a moment. The bump. Everything went black."

"I know a little of that feeling," Maggie said. "Let's check you out, Pearl."

"Don't worry! I called 911." At the sound of a familiar voice, Maggie looked toward Sedgwick Manor and saw that Ina had hobbled onto the front stoop, her ubiquitous pencil and notepad in hand. *Oh no.*

Just a few minutes later, two more police cars, an ambulance, and a fire truck arrived one after the other.

Maggie was able to get Pearl out of her VW and helped her sit down next to Maxine and Harriet on the curb. Two EMTs kneeled down in front of them and checked their vitals. After several minutes, the three stood up, brushed themselves off, and said the most curious thing in unison.

"Fit as a fiddle."

Then they looked at one another and chuckled a bit—even literal-to-the-bone Pearl, for whom Maggie thought the colloquial phrase was quite atypical.

Officer Samantha Clayton appeared in front of them with a clipboard. "Ladies, I will need to get some identification from you for an accident report."

Maggie groaned. "I hope no one gets a ticket for what happened here today. I would feel awful."

Officer Linton, standing nearby, blushed a little. "The customary rule in a situation like this is the driver in the car from behind is at fault. Technically that's me. But the ladies here were backing up without looking."

"But they thought all was clear behind them," Maggie said.

"Rules are rules, I'm afraid," Officer Clayton said. "We've got to do this by the book, especially since there's another officer involved."

Pearl, Harriet, and Maxine all approached Officer Clayton with their driver's licenses. One by one, she wrote down their identification and contact information. As the officer filled out several forms, she got a confused look on her face. "Wow," she said. "Did you three know you all have the exact same birthday? Seventy-five years ago today."

Maxine, Harriet, and Pearl exchanged glances silently.

"Let me see those," Maxine said, grabbing the licenses from the other two women. "The same birth date? What are the odds?"

Then they spoke over one another.

"Well, I'll be," Maxine said, frowning.

"My goodness," Harriet said, hands on her hips.

"That is hard to believe," Pearl said in practically a whisper.

Maggie stepped into the group. "This is too crazy. Where were you all born?"

They answered in unison: "Ellsmith-by-the-Bay, Massachusetts." Their eyes widened as they exchanged glances.

"And who were your parents?" Maggie asked.

One by one, each of the women admitted she had never known her birth parents.

As Maggie looked at the three tall women standing next to one another, she began to notice other similarities: warm brown eyes, a strong nose, and a wide mouth with thin lips. How had she not seen this before, even with the mystery of the dress?

"Should I say it?" Maggie asked. "I think there's a strong possibility you're sisters. Triplets. Separated at birth."

Everyone was quiet for a moment as the idea sunk in.

And then Pearl spoke. "I know what happened. I know the story."

19

Half an hour later, the cars were cleared out of the street and Maggie had bid farewell to the police officers and the EMTs. Robert had said what he'd come by to tell her wasn't urgent, so she promised to call him later in the afternoon. Maura had returned to the public library, telling Pearl she was sorry to miss her story but that she expected all the details later. Harriet had called Shelby at A Fine Vintage to let her know she'd be awhile longer still. Maxine had checked her website to verify that she had no bookings for the afternoon. Magenta had retreated to the kitchen to clean up the lunch dishes. And Ruth had driven Ina home, ignoring Ina's protests about getting the details of the triplets' story for the society column.

All that remained was to hear Pearl's story.

Maggie settled everyone in the living room with more tea, and the air crackled with nervous energy. She couldn't wait to hear the origin of this story, how three women, so different and yet so similar, had been separated for nearly seventy-five years only to be reunited under the most coincidental of circumstances.

Maggie cleared her throat. "Before we get started with Pearl's story, I have to tell you ladies something." She tried to keep a straight face.

"What?" they said together, then grinned at one another.

"I'm upset that none of you told me you had a birthday today," Maggie said. "I would have had cake for dessert."

They all had a good laugh together.

"As a matter of fact, I agreed to come because it's my birthday and I didn't have any other plans," Harriet said, smoothing her skirt across her knees.

"I never did much celebrating," Maxine said. "I figure one day's the same as the next. But when you invited me, I thought for sure you somehow knew today was my—our birthday."

"I'm still trying to wrap my head around this odd coincidence," Maggie said. "I think it's time for Pearl to tell us what she knows about your family."

Pearl took a deep breath, then began stringing more words together than Maggie suspected she had said in the last month.

"I don't know what you two thought," she began, looking at Harriet and Maxine, "but I always wondered why my birth parents didn't want me. Or why they couldn't keep me, which I suppose was another option, though I never paid it much mind. Consumed with the desire to know about my birth parents, I spent all of my downtime at the library researching them. And what I found out . . ."

Pearl paused, and the other women leaned toward her, all on the edges of their seats. "It's a sad love story," Pearl continued. And she told the tale as though she were reading aloud from one of the Gothic romances she cherished.

. . . .

Edna Stanfield and John Richmond were the definition of an all-American couple. They grew up in Boston, and both enjoyed the privileges that came with belonging to two quite well-to-do families. Not obscenely rich, but comfortable. Despite both being barely eighteen, John proposed to Edna with a delicate white gold ring on the Fourth of July, 1928, and her parents were prepared to give her the most extravagant wedding either family had ever seen the following spring.

On the eve of the wedding, however, Edna's parents learned that John's father had swindled them in a financial scheme, and the Stanfields were ruined. Edna's father forbade her to marry John. Undeterred, she sent John a note asking him to meet her at the church the next morning. She wanted them to be wed with or without her father's permission. He responded immediately that he would be there no matter what. He placed what was to be her wedding ring in the envelope with his letter, saying that he couldn't wait another minute for her to have it.

The following morning, Edna dressed herself in her custom-made gown and snuck out of the house, arriving at the church only to see John driving away from it. Some newspaper photographers, journalists, and society columnists had already gathered for the wedding they didn't know was canceled, and the photographers captured several images of Edna chasing after John, freshly heartbroken. Rumor has it that when Edna stopped chasing the car, she tore the veil from her head and ripped it from bottom to top in anguish.

John sent her only one other note, to say that after much contemplation, he was off to seek a life and a fortune that was his alone, so her father would once again give his permission for them to marry. Edna waited a month, a year, a decade, but John never returned.

Her family moved to the small fishing village of Ellsmith-by-the-Bay in 1933, but Edna held out hope for nearly a decade after that John would find her, save her from her solitary existence. Her family had fallen far, and she helped make ends meet by serving at the local drugstore counter. One day, a young man named Jimmy Taylor swooped into town looking for a job and a good time, not necessarily in that order. He was ten or more years her junior, and he'd avoided the draft with a failed physical. One of the first days he was in town, he met Edna at the drugstore. He quickly convinced her that she needed a husband, that she was too old to be picky. The truth was that he just needed a place to live and someone to take care of him. They married a month later. In nine months he was gone, and she was left with newborn triplets.

When her parents died a short time after, Edna was all alone and practically penniless. Completely crushed and destitute, she gave up her three-month-old girls so they could have a better life. The girls went to three separate families, and the families lost track of one another. Like seeds on the wind, the babies drifted far and wide.

.   .   .   .

Pearl sighed when she finished telling her story.

Maxine got her wallet out of her pants pocket and found the newspaper clipping she had shown Maggie. "I've carried this around since I was a child, always wondering who it was. And now I know. This is our mother, in the wedding dress she never used. At least I'm guessing she never used it, since it was many years later when she finally married."

Harriet and Maxine looked at the photo together. "She must have been so sad," Harriet said. "Losing the fiancé she loved, then her husband, then her parents, then giving up her babies. It's almost as if she gave you this clipping so you'd see it and know how sad she was. As if she thought giving us up was the only way to make sure we were never sad like her."

Maggie watched the sisters, Maxine in her utilitarian navy twill and Harriet in her silky gray dress, their shoulders touching as they sat beside each other and talked about the photograph. *They may have an explanation for why Maxine has that photo, but I still don't know why there was a similar one in Aunt Evelyn's album.*

Maggie was about to mention her copy of the picture when Maxine grimaced and said, "I'd like to slug that man—our father—for leaving our mother." She looked first at Pearl, then at Harriet. "We could have been together all these years if he hadn't walked out on her."

"We can't help what happened," Harriet said. "The past is the past. We will just have to make up for it now. Isn't it curious that we all ended up in Somerset Harbor? And here at Maggie's house on our birthday?"

The other two nodded in agreement.

As Pearl stared at the photo, her face seemed softer to Maggie. "Such a beautiful dress," Pearl said. "Too bad it's gone."

"Yes," Maggie said, "too bad it's gone. Now that I know this story, I would have given it to you three ladies. And did you know I also had the matching veil?"

"Her veil?" Harriet stiffened.

"Yes, it was in the same package as the dress. It was torn, so I kept it here at the house. I even considered getting it repaired—but it was stolen last night."

No one spoke, and the quiet sat heavy in the room for many moments.

"You know," Maggie said, breaking the silence, "I still don't understand why Aunt Evelyn had that dress in the first place. Hopefully now that the truth is coming out in the open, I will not only find out the connection with Aunt Evelyn but find out who took the dress and the veil."

It seemed to Maggie that each of the women looked uncomfortable. She decided not to mention the rings—they were evidence she wanted to keep as quiet as possible. And she certainly did not want them to go missing too.

Besides, they could provide a means to check out one last possibility.

. . . .

After the ladies left, Maggie found Magenta reading a large hardcover book at the breakfast table. "You did a great job cleaning up, Magenta," she said, gesturing toward her sparkling-clean kitchen.

The girl nodded. "I'm sorry for running out on you earlier," Magenta said. "I almost didn't come, but I'm glad I did."

"I'm glad you came too. Did you happen to overhear any of that conversation?"

Magenta smiled a little. "I didn't mean to eavesdrop, but wow, what a story. It was like a book."

"I only wish Edna could have had a happier ending." Maggie paused for a moment, then said, "Magenta, I want to show you something. Come with me."

Maggie led Magenta into her bedroom. She picked up the polished wooden jewelry box and opened it. "Ode to Joy" tinkled as Maggie lifted the two rings and put them into Magenta's palm.

"Wow," Magenta said, holding up the rings to look them over. "These are beautiful." She looked at Maggie. "Whose are they?" She tried them on her finger and admired them.

"I'm guessing they were Edna Stanfield's," Maggie said. "I found them in the pocket of the wedding dress. They must be the rings that John Richmond gave to her."

Magenta took them off and handed them back to Maggie. "Any girl would be lucky to get those." Magenta's expression was somber, and Maggie wondered if it was because Magenta was feeling guilty or because she was contemplating the rings' sad history.

Maggie put the rings back into the jewelry box and set it back on her dresser. Part of her was loathe to even think it, but if Magenta was the one who had taken the dress and veil, she might also take the rings. Only a few people knew about them. If the rings disappeared, Magenta would probably be the thief. She had been helpful this week, that was certain, but much of her behavior struck Maggie as odd. Even for a teenager.

"Magenta," Maggie said, "do you think you could stay and run the vacuum? I'd like to check in with June at the shop. You can let yourself out when you're done."

"Sure, no problem," Magenta said, heading for the pantry to get the vacuum.

Maggie left out the side door and took the wooded path to the antiques shop. Along the way, her thoughts returned to Magenta's behavior the past week as she tried to justify her own suspicions and the trap she'd just set. Magenta was a girl who noticed the tiniest of details, so she must have seen the veil in Maggie's bedroom when she gave her a tour of the house. Who else had been in Sedgwick Manor? True, Magenta had told her about seeing someone, presumably Harriet, carry a white dress into the back entrance of A Fine Vintage. But Magenta was smart, and she could easily have been trying to divert Maggie's attention away from herself.

If Magenta had taken the veil or the dress, she might also take the rings. Leaving the girl alone at the manor would give her the perfect opportunity to do just that—but Maggie hoped against hope that she wouldn't.

When Maggie entered the shop, June was busy at the counter, helping a young couple purchase a primitive dough table. After the couple carried the table out the front door to their waiting SUV, Maggie filled June in on the story of the triplet sisters.

"That's incredible," June said. "And now the three of them are all living here. This should be on television, don't you think? There's a show now that documents these kinds of reunions."

"I'm still reeling from the whole thing," Maggie said.

"Just imagine, if you hadn't had your luncheon, they might never have known. They should frame their traffic citations."

"I guess they can tell people they just happened to run into each other," Maggie said with a twinkle in her eye. "Which is true."

June laughed, but as she did, her gaze landed on the window

display, and her mirth faded. "I still feel bad about the dress. Have you or Robert made any progress on finding it?"

"No, and I didn't even get a chance to tell you yet that the veil was stolen last night too." Maggie told June about the intruder, being knocked out, and talking to Officer Linton that morning. "Actually, I think he was coming by to update me on the investigation when the world's most fateful traffic accident occurred. I need to give him a call."

"Are you feeling okay now?" June's brow was furrowed in concern. "With a bump on the head and a busy morning, you should really take it easy. I've got things under control here. Why don't you go rest up?"

"Nothing crazy going on here today?"

"No, just Liz and Pastor David coming by to pick up the items for the Old Faith tag sale. Other than that, business as usual. I hope."

"I might go get a cup of coffee and take the rest of the day to finish reading *Jane Eyre* then."

June nodded. "Sounds like just what the doctor ordered."

They said goodbye, and Maggie headed toward The Busy Bean. As she walked, she dialed Robert's cell number. He picked up on the third ring. "Hello, Maggie. Long time no talk."

"Hey, Robert. Any news on the investigation?" Maggie asked.

"Unfortunately, no," he said. "I was coming by earlier to let you know that the fingerprints I pulled from the note didn't match anything in the database."

"So that means whoever wrote the note doesn't have a criminal record?"

"I don't think it's a stretch to say we're not dealing with a professional burglar here," Robert said. "I'm back to piecing together Maxine's garbage."

Maggie thanked him, wished him luck, and disconnected the call as she reached The Busy Bean. She saw not one but four familiar faces through the café window. James was at Maggie's favorite table overlooking the harbor, engrossed in a newspaper. At the next table sat three women who, until today, Maggie would have never expected to see dining together: Maxine, Harriet, and Pearl.

When Maggie entered the café, she saw that James was still fully focused on his newspaper, so she walked over to the three sisters.

"Maggie," Harriet said brightly, "can we buy you a cup of coffee? It's the least we can do for your hospitality earlier today."

Maggie started to protest, but Maxine held up her hand.

"I've already got it," Maxine said, standing up and looking around the café. She waved to Jenny the waitress and called across the room, "French roast, biggest size you have."

Jenny gave them a thumbs-up.

"Thank you," Maggie said, taking an empty seat next to Harriet as Maxine sat down. "So Pearl, you were the one who had the whole story. I'd love to hear about how you pieced it all together."

"I started by reading newspapers from Ellsmith-by-the-Bay from the year I—we were born," Pearl said. "I found our birth announcement, and then our grandparents' obituaries, and then I traced it back from there."

"But you never tried to find your sisters?" Maggie leaned toward Pearl as Jenny placed a cup of coffee in front of her and slipped away.

"Our names were all changed when we went to our new homes," Pearl said. "My parents told me what my birth name was when I started asking questions years and years ago, but they didn't know my sisters' adopted names. And the adoption agency's office burned down in the 1950s, so all of our records were gone. I had no way to track them down."

"And my adopted family had to give me up. It would have been nearly impossible to find me in foster care," Maxine added.

"How did you learn about Edna's first engagement?" Maggie asked.

"Stanfield was an important-enough name in Boston in the 1920s, and it was a big deal in the social columns at the time. I saw Maxine's newspaper clipping during my research. They put that picture of Mother looking so sad in the paper—can you believe it?"

"Rather tasteless if you ask me," Harriet said with a sniff.

At the next table, James looked up from his newspaper and caught Maggie's eye. She waved and held up her index finger to indicate she'd come over in a moment. "Ladies, I'm so thrilled you found each other, truly."

"We wouldn't have ever figured it out if you hadn't had us over for lunch," Pearl said. "Thank you."

"You're always welcome at my home, Pearl," Maggie said. "All of you. I feel like we're family somehow. Though I suppose we still have some work to do, figuring out how your mother's dress ended up in my aunt's closet."

"Another day, I suppose," Harriet said. "I've had about as many revelations today as I can handle."

The sisters decided it was time to take their reunion home—to Pearl's house, it sounded like—so Maggie thanked Maxine again for the coffee and excused herself to talk to James.

"Hope I'm not interrupting," she said, nodding toward his paper. "I have some crazy news to share."

"You're never an interruption," James said. "Have a seat and tell me all."

Maggie sat down across from James, then spent the next half hour telling him about the luncheon, the accident, and the discovery about the three women.

Every so often, James would get a stunned look on his face and interject, "Triplets?"

Her response each time was "Yes, triplets."

After the story about the sisters, the conversation turned again to the stolen wedding dress and veil, and the wedding rings. She confessed to James that she had essentially set Magenta up by showing her the rings. "I'm completely at loose ends with these thefts," she said. "I don't want to suspect Magenta, but I also don't want to think Maxine, Harriet, or Pearl is responsible either."

"You're in a tough spot," James said. "But why would Magenta have stolen the dress or the veil in the first place? Honestly, if she steals the rings, it could just be because they're valuable."

Maggie sagged in her seat. "You have a point."

"Why don't I come back to the house with you for moral support?" James asked. "No time like the present."

With a wave to Daisy, Maggie and James left The Busy Bean and walked the few blocks to Sedgwick Manor. As they approached the manor, Maggie caught a glimpse of Snickers crouched on the ground near the sidewalk, watching something in the bushes with rapt attention.

When they got to the front door, James held his hand up. "Maggie, this time *I'll* open the door. No more surprises, no more accidents."

Maggie smiled and gave a mock salute. "Yes sir."

However, no one rushed out toward them as he turned the handle. "So far, so good," he said with a grin.

Maggie shook a finger at him. "Are you making fun of me?"

"Never."

They walked into the foyer of Sedgwick Manor.

"Magenta?" Maggie called out. No answer.

James peeked into the dining room, and Maggie looked in the library and then the adjoining office. All quiet.

As they walked into the kitchen, James asked, "So where would the rings be?"

"I left them in a jewelry box on my dresser," Maggie said. "I'll go get it." She walked to the dresser in her room, picked up the polished box, and opened it as she approached James. The rings were there, just as she had left them.

"So Magenta didn't take them," James said. "That's good, right?"

"Absolutely." Maggie nodded. "Except now I'm back at square one, with a missing dress and a missing veil, and no idea about who could have taken them. One person? Two people? And that note that said the dress was still in town. What was that all about?"

All of a sudden they heard a faint creaking, followed by what sounded like something rolling across a floor.

Maggie froze. "Did you hear that, James?" she whispered.

"Yes. Is it the cat?"

"I just saw him outside in the bushes."

"A mouse, then? Let's wait a minute, see if we hear it again."

They both stood silently, listening.

Within moments, they heard it again.

"It's upstairs," Maggie whispered. "Will you come with me? And bring the fireplace poker?"

"Fireplace poker?" James asked. "If it's a mouse, I'd rather have a broom."

Maggie tiptoed to the pantry and got a broom. Then she walked to the living room fireplace, grabbed the poker, and handed it to James while keeping the broom for herself. "Just in case."

As quietly as possible, they headed up the curved staircase to the second floor and stood silently on the landing.

"Listen," Maggie said. "I hear it again. I think it's coming from the attic. James, the attic. Just like in *Jane Eyre*."

James smiled. "Or perhaps you just have a family of mice."

Maggie shook her head and pointed to the attic door. She opened the door slowly and crept up the stairs. When she reached the top of the steps, she nearly gasped at the truly unexpected scene in front of her.

Pearl sat in an old rocking chair in the middle of the attic.

And she was wearing the stolen wedding veil and dress.

20

"Pearl," Maggie said gently, "what are you doing?" Pearl bounded out of the rocking chair, which made the same creaking sound Maggie and James had heard, only louder now that they were in the same room. "I . . . I . . ." Pearl stuttered a bit, then swallowed, took a deep breath, and spoke clearly. "I was bringing the veil back to you, and I found the dress on your front steps, folded neatly. I didn't take either of them, but I remembered what you said earlier this afternoon—that the dress, if it were found, should belong to my sisters and me."

"But you just said that you were bringing *back* the veil," James said. "I don't understand."

"Someone else took the veil," Pearl said. "I don't want to say who did it, because she—I mean, that person could get in trouble."

"Okay," Maggie said, "but why are you in my attic?"

Pearl looked a bit sheepish. "Have you read *Jane Eyre* yet, Maggie?"

"Mostly. But what does that have to do with anything?"

"I mean, you said I was always welcome in your home—to come by anytime. We're sort of family, right? So here I am. I thought that for maybe just a few moments I could be a real-life character like one in a Brontë novel. I guess it was kind of silly, but I never got to play much make-believe as a child." Pearl glanced down at the floor, then back up at Maggie and James. "Our mother's story is much like one of those Gothic heroines, you know. She married a tragic figure who left her with grief on her hands. I was trying to connect with her, trying to imagine how she felt."

"Pearl," Maggie said, "I imagine that your mother loved you all very much but was just overwhelmed and wanted the best for you. As it turns out, your story is not one of sadness. You have a happy ending, with your sisters. Right?"

Pearl nodded.

James cleared his throat. "Maggie, the writer of the note was right. The dress *was* in town—the veil too. And now you have them both back. Case solved."

"Except—" Maggie cut off when she heard the doorbell faintly ringing from two stories below. "And now someone is at the front door. Let's all just go downstairs. All right, Pearl?"

Pearl started down the stairs after James. She was still wearing the wedding dress over her street clothes, but Maggie figured a few more minutes wouldn't hurt anything. The doorbell rang again.

Moments later they were all in the foyer, and Maggie opened the door to find Maxine and Harriet.

"Pearl, what are you doing?" Maxine asked, aghast.

"This wasn't the plan, Pearl," Harriet added.

"The plan?" James chimed in.

Maggie gestured toward the living room. "Let's all sit down again, please."

Once everyone was seated, Maggie crossed her arms. "Now let's start at the beginning."

Despite all three sisters repeatedly interrupting one another, the story quickly unfolded. The day that Harriet and Maxine had first visited Carriage House Antiques, they both knew they wanted the dress. It was Harriet, though, who had gone back to the shop that morning after the storms with the intention of borrowing the dress to make a pattern of it so that she could sew her own version.

"When I saw that June was busy with another customer,"

Harriet said, "I just looked around for a while. I was also fascinated with a beautiful tapestry that I thought I could use in A Fine Vintage. I was looking it over when I saw June take some photos and then leave the shop."

"Did you happen to be behind the tapestry?" Maggie asked.

"Probably," Harriet said. "I did look on the back to check the quality of the stitching before I decided how much I'd be willing to pay for it."

"So how did you end up with the dress?" Maggie was glad that at least she now knew whose eyes were in June's photo, but she still had a million questions to go before she was truly satisfied.

"I took the dress off the mannequin and thought I could get to my shop, sketch out a pattern, and return the dress before anyone really noticed." Harriet shrugged. "I guess I was wrong. It turned out to be a trickier pattern than I expected. I truly didn't intend to keep it."

However, as Harriet headed back toward her shop, she almost ran into Maxine, who was riding her transporter down the alley behind A Fine Vintage. In a huff, Maxine had stormed over to chew Harriet out, and she noticed that she was carrying the dress. Ever the rule follower, Maxine went to Sedgwick Manor to tell Maggie who had the dress—in the hopes that Maggie would then recover it and let Maxine have it.

"But when I got to your door, I wondered which was worse, a thief or a tattletale, so I left without saying anything."

"You must have been the person James saw that afternoon," Maggie said.

Maxine sat straight with her hands on her knees. "The next day, I drove my car—yes, I have a car—over to Harriet's shop and took the dress from the back room, thinking I'd find the right time to bring it back to you."

"Maxine, I think I actually was in the back room when you took the dress," Maggie said, blushing.

Harriet stood up, indignant. "You were *both* in the back room of my store? But—"

Maggie touched Harriet on the arm. "I apologize, I was just trying to find my dress."

Harriet's bluster melted away. "I'm not exactly an innocent party here. After all, I did take a dress off a mannequin in your display window." She sat back down, crossed her ankles, and carefully spread her skirt across her knees.

Before anyone else could speak, the doorbell rang yet again. Maggie went to the door and swung it open to reveal her latest unexpected guest. It was Magenta.

She had her head down, pink-tipped hair hanging loose in front of her slumped shoulders. "I did something wrong."

"Okay," Maggie said, "but can it wait until I straighten out another mess?"

Magenta looked up at her with watery eyes. "Does it have to do with the missing veil?"

"Yes it does," Maggie said, getting the sense that Magenta would provide another piece of the puzzle. "Why don't you join us?" She ushered Magenta into the living room. "So, where were we? Maxine, you said you stole the dress from Harriet's shop and that you *planned* to return the dress to me. Why didn't you?"

"Every time I looked for an opportunity to return it, I would see you. I didn't want you to think I had stolen it."

Maggie raised her eyebrows. "Did you have it in one of those black plastic bags?"

"Yes. But for the record, I do carry my laundry to and from the laundromat in garbage bags."

"Try to stay on subject, Maxine," Pearl said.

"Right. After a couple tries, it became easier to just keep the dress. You may have noticed I was avoiding you."

"The thought crossed my mind."

"I felt bad, so I wrote you the note about the dress still being in town."

"Ah." Maggie now knew where she recognized that handwriting from—it was similar to Maxine's business signs.

"I didn't want you to worry," Maxine said. "You're a nice person, Maggie, and you brought us together. So when we sisters met for coffee, before you got there, of course, Harriet and I explained to Pearl about the dress. We agreed we would return it. And that's when we learned about the veil."

"The veil?" Maggie asked.

"I'm afraid that's where I come in," Magenta said from the corner of the room. "Yesterday I found another book about 1920s fashion, and Aunt Maura asked me to bring it to you after we closed. But when I got here, no one answered the doorbell. I tried the knob, and it was unlocked. So instead of leaving the book on the steps, I thought I'd put it on the table in the foyer. But I never even took it out of my backpack, because that's when I did the first dumb thing."

"Go on," Maggie said.

"I remembered the bridal veil and thought it would be cool to take pictures of myself in it." Magenta shrugged. "Then I did the second dumb thing."

"Which was?" Maggie was starting to figure out where the girl's story was going.

Magenta twisted her hair with her fingers. "I wanted to take a picture, but my phone was dead, so I plugged in my charging cord in the bathroom. I guess the end of the cord got water on it from the sink or something, because when I plugged in the phone, the lights went out."

Maggie shook her head. "You could have been electrocuted, Magenta."

Magenta bit her lower lip nervously. "The third dumb thing I did was run out of the house. By that time, I was so on edge I forgot I had the veil on. And when I opened the door, I ran right into you."

"Ah," Maggie said, and then let out a breath.

"And I kept going." Magenta's voice grew tearful. "Halfway down the block I realized I still had the veil on. I never meant to steal it, honest, but I was afraid of what you'd think if you knew I'd been in your house like that."

"I couldn't think, Magenta. You knocked me out."

"I didn't realize," Magenta said. "I just ran as fast as I could. I'm so sorry, Maggie. I want to make this up to you somehow. I was going to bring it back, but then I couldn't find it, and I really didn't know what to do."

Pearl cleared her throat. "I think I can finish this story."

"You can?" Maggie looked at Pearl in surprise.

"Magenta hid the veil in a backpack that she took to work at the library," Pearl said. "Yesterday morning, I saw the backpack in the break room. The zipper was undone a little, and I saw the veil inside. I took it out and immediately recognized it as the one I had overheard Maggie talking about."

"And what did you do with it?" Maggie's head hurt, and not simply from the bump she'd gotten the night before.

"I won't lie," Pearl continued. "I was intrigued by the idea of the veil being ripped—like the one that had belonged to Jane Eyre—so I kept it. Like Maxine, I fully intended to return it to you, Maggie. But also like Maxine, I felt drawn to it in a way that I could not understand."

"But when she told us about it, we made her agree to return it, as Maxine promised to return the dress," Harriet said.

"I kept up my end of the bargain," Maxine chimed in.

"I did too," Pearl said. "Or I tried to. I intended to leave it on the steps with Maxine's package, but when I saw the dress, I got carried away." She looked down at herself, still wearing the gown and the veil over her street clothes. She finally removed them and draped them carefully over an empty chair nearby.

Maggie shook her head. "I don't know what to say. Or do."

James, who had been sitting and listening quietly the entire time, said, "They're all guilty in some way or another, Maggie, but they're also quite innocent. And now you have the dress, the veil, and the rings."

"What rings?" the three sisters said together.

"Hold tight," Maggie said, then dashed from the room. She retrieved the rings from the jewelry box in her bedroom and brought them out to the living room. "These fell out of the pocket of the dress the morning I brought it to Carriage House Antiques. I'm assuming they were your mother's—the ring that her fiancé had given her in 1928, and the one he gave her with his letter agreeing to meet her at the church. The rings are inscribed *E & J.* Edna and John."

Maggie handed them to Harriet, who examined them from every angle and then gave them to Maxine, who was sitting next to her on the sofa.

"They're lovely," Harriet said, her voice almost reverent. "These would get a pretty penny."

"Most pennies are rather unattractive, in my opinion," Pearl interjected from an adjacent chair.

"We are *not* selling our mother's rings," Maxine said firmly. "I've never seen anything so beautiful." Seemingly reluctant, she passed them to Pearl.

"Technically, the rings are not ours," Pearl said, handing them back to Maggie. "They're Maggie's. They would be beautiful on her someday, as would the wedding dress. And I understand she has a daughter."

For what felt like the umpteenth time that day, the doorbell rang.

"It's Aunt Maura," Magenta said. "I asked her to come over so I could explain things."

Maggie pocketed the rings and started to leave to answer the door, but James said, "Let me."

A few moments later, James returned with Maura. As she went over to Magenta, he approached Maggie. "I feel a bit like a fifth wheel here, or even sixth or seventh," he said quietly. "I think I'll leave you to it."

"Are you sure?" Maggie asked with a smile. "Who knows what else you'll miss?"

James chuckled, then wished everyone well and left.

Maura spoke up. "I came as soon as I got Magenta's message. What's going on?"

Magenta took a deep breath. "I need to tell you something, Aunt Maura. I did something wrong. Something for which I am very sorry."

Maggie watched Magenta and Maura as the young girl weepily recounted her accidental thievery.

Maura had one arm across her chest, hand resting in the crook of the opposite elbow. The fingers of the other hand rested on her temple as she listened without interrupting. When Magenta had finished her confession, the librarian appeared to be weighing her words. When she spoke, she did so to Maggie instead of her niece. "Maggie, I am humiliated by and most sorry for what occurred. While I know you have the veil back in your possession, Magenta needs to understand that there are consequences for one's actions."

"Aunt Maura, I—" Magenta started to protest, but her aunt gestured for her to stop.

"How do you think you could redeem this situation?" Maura asked Magenta. "What could you do to make it up to Maggie?"

Maggie wanted to say that it was all right—that she was fine, the veil was back, and there was no harm done. But she knew that this could be an important lesson for Magenta. She looked at the teen, whose eyes were still wide and damp.

"Maggie, it was wrong for me to go into your home and take something that was not mine—no matter my intentions. Will you forgive me?"

Maggie looked at the young girl with her arms wrapped around her midsection, holding herself tightly. She was suffering from much in her life she could not control. She needed grace.

"Of course, Magenta. Come here."

Magenta moved toward her, and Maggie gave her a big hug.

Seemingly softening, Maura said, "Forgiveness is fine, but I think there ought to be some sort of restitution." She walked over to her niece and embraced her as well. "I care about you, Magenta. I just want you to take responsibility for your actions."

The girl thought for a moment, then smiled a little. "What if I keep working for Maggie, but do it for free?"

Maggie nodded. "I think that sounds like the perfect solution. Maura?"

"It's fine with me if it's okay with you."

Maggie looked around the room. "And I'll ask Officer Linton to drop any charges relating to the missing dress and veil. It's up to the police department, of course. But as far as I am concerned, the case is closed. Except for one thing." She sighed. "We still don't know the reason Aunt Evelyn had the dress, the veil, and the rings."

Everyone was quiet for several moments. Magenta hesitantly

approached the dress and touched the beading on the neckline gently. She looked up. "What did you say Edna's last name was?"

"Stanfield," Pearl said. "Why?"

An enormous smile lit up the teenager's face. "Follow me."

Maggie, Maura, and the triplets trailed Magenta to the library, where the girl marched to the rolling ladder and climbed it swiftly. She examined an upper shelf for a moment, then pulled out a leather-bound book. It was the copy of *Jane Eyre* she'd discovered while organizing the books. She held it high in triumph, then descended the ladder. She opened the front cover. "'To my heroic second cousin Franklin, whose generosity goes unmatched,'" Magenta read aloud. "'You are the beginning and the end of our relationship with J.P. May a woman of Sedgwick Manor find use for these, as no Stanfield ever will.' The inscription is signed, 'Peter Stanfield, October 24, 1931.'"

"But what does it mean?" Maggie reached for the book as Magenta held it out to her. "Was he talking about this copy of *Jane Eyre*?"

Magenta let go of the book before Maggie had it in her grasp, and it fell to the floor, open to a page in the middle. A yellowed piece of paper fluttered to the ground nearby.

The women exchanged glances. Maxine bent down and picked up the paper, then read it, first to herself, then aloud. "It's a bill of sale. 'One Jean Patierre bridal dress, mint condition. $1,000. One matching veil, in need of repair. $50. One white gold engagement and wedding ring set. $500. One first-edition *Jane Eyre*. $300. Sold to Franklin Sedgwick by Peter Stanfield.' Signed by both men and dated October 24, 1931."

"Franklin Sedgwick was my great-grandfather," Maggie said. "He hosted extravagant Independence Day parties here in the '20s. Edna and John must have been the couple Jean Patierre met on the Fourth of July who inspired him to design the wedding dress.

I'm guessing Peter was Edna's father." She retrieved the 1920s family album from a nearby shelf and pulled out the photo of Edna wearing the dress.

"Yes, Peter Stanfield was our grandfather," Pearl said. She gestured toward the album Maggie held. "What's that?"

"I'm sorry I never mentioned this," Maggie said, "but I did find this photo while I was looking for information on the dress. I think it's the original of Maxine's newspaper clipping. It was in the back of the album, not set in place like the rest of the photos." She handed it to Pearl.

Pearl stared intently at the image for a moment, then turned it over. She inhaled sharply. "'Photographed by Ralph Finn.' Ralph Finn was a society photographer for *The Boston Times*. I recognize his name from when I researched our parents."

"Maybe this photo came with the bill of sale and just got tucked into an album by a later relative," Harriet said as Pearl handed her the photograph.

"That seems likely," Maggie said.

Harriet and Maxine traded documents and continued their examinations. Maxine pulled her newspaper clipping out and looked at the photos side by side. "They look the same," she said, then set them on a table where everyone could see them.

Harriet examined the bill of sale in her hand. "Pearl, you said the Stanfields were swindled by John Richmond's father, right?"

"Yes, and what they had left they lost in the market crash."

"I'd have to ask June, but those dollar amounts seem a little inflated to me for that era," Maggie said. "Do you think that maybe my great-grandfather bought the dress and the book to help bail out his second cousin?"

"That seems fairly likely." Harriet examined the paper again. "Why else would he have paid so much for a book? Not to mention a dress that would soon be out of style and a torn veil."

"The family must have sold off everything they owned, bit by bit," Maxine said. "I bet our mother fought tooth and nail to keep them from selling her wedding gown. But desperate times call for desperate measures, I guess."

"They moved to Ellsmith-by-the-Bay in 1933," Pearl said. "That must have been when the money ran out and they finally lost their Boston house."

Maxine looked at her sisters, then turned to Maggie. "I think this is proof that the dress is yours, Maggie. The dress, the veil, the rings. Everything."

Maggie shook her head vigorously. "No. I can't possibly keep them now. They belong to you triplets. Truly."

At once, a heated discussion started about who was the rightful owner. After a minute or two of fervent argument, a whistle pierced the air.

Maura removed her fingers from her mouth and put her hands on her hips. "I think I have a solution that will work for everyone. Harriet, you already have an impressive collection of wedding dresses on display at A Fine Vintage. Perhaps it would make sense for you to put the dress and veil in your window. That way, you can see it every day, and Maxine and Pearl can see it anytime they come by. As for the rings, there are two of them. The other sisters can each take one so everyone has something."

"But I wouldn't feel right separating the rings from each other," Maxine said in protest. "They belong together."

"Besides, who would get which one?" Pearl asked.

"And honestly, it's a little unfair that I'm getting two items in this deal," Harriet chimed in.

Maggie thought for a moment, then smiled. "You're forgetting the book. Pearl, would you like this copy of *Jane Eyre* that belonged to your mother's family? Would it be okay for

Maxine to have the rings and you to take this book?"

Pearl closed her eyes for a moment, then opened them. Maggie had never seen such delight in the older woman's expression, not even when she'd been enjoying her dessert earlier. "If I had this book, I'd be—"

"—fit as a fiddle!" her sisters finished with her.

Everyone laughed.

· · · · · · · · · · · · · · · · ·

A few days later, Maggie retrieved her weekly copy of *The Somerset Harbor Herald* from the front steps and carried it to the breakfast table. As she sipped her coffee, she paged through the newspaper. When she got to the society column, she froze. Then she smiled.

Somerset Harbor Social Happenings

By Ina Linton

On June 8, Harriet Hamstead hosted an opening day reception at her new store, A Fine Vintage. Ladies of all ages shopped for high-quality classic fashions while nibbling on scones, courtesy of Mrs. Daisy Carter at The Busy Bean, and admiring Ms. Hamstead's museum-quality collection of antique wedding gowns.

On June 9, the members of the Somerset Harbor Historical Society feted Ruth Harper in honor of her fifteen years of noble service as society president. The other members presented her with a plaque and a scrapbook commemorating her many achievements and the countless fund-raisers she has helmed.

On June 10, the Somerset Harbor Senior Center held
their Dancing With the Seniors competition at the VFW
hall. Despite his talented partner's devastating last-minute
injury, former professional dancer Ernest Streeter and his
substitute partner, Harriet Hamstead, won first place with
a charming Charleston. We wish his injured partner all the
best on her recovery.

On June 11, Maggie Watson of Carriage House Antiques
hosted a luncheon for several recently retired women new
to Somerset Harbor. In the course of the luncheon, Harriet
Hamstead (A Fine Vintage), Maxine MacDonald (Lean On
Me Tours), and Pearl Winters (Somerset Harbor Public
Library) discovered they were long-lost triplets. Certainly,
one is never too old for a new beginning.

Maggie sat back and looked out the window at the bright
June morning. Snickers hopped into her lap and began to purr.
She couldn't agree with Ina more.

Up to this point, we've been doing all the writing. Now it's *your* turn!

Tell us what you think about this book, the characters, the bad guy, or anything else you'd like to share with us about this series. We can't wait to hear from *you*!

Log on to give us your feedback at:
https://www.surveymonkey.com/r/AntiqueShop

Annie's® FICTION